DELIVERING A GOOD TIME

by Frank Sol

Chapter One

I opened my eyes when the alarm clicked on. I couldn't stand the buzzing sound—it would set my nerves on edge for hours—and relied on the radio. The insipid melody of the latest bubblegum pop singer was enough to wake me from even the deepest sleep.

It was Saturday and I wanted to just stay and sleep, but I had work to do.

I owned a duplex and lived in the right-side half while renting out the left side. The rental pretty much paid the mortgage and enough of the various carrying costs that I actually didn't have to worry too much about things.

Oh, I'd heard plenty of horror stories about problem tenants and the like, but I never had any problem with anyone I'd rented too.

Maybe I was just lucky that way.

Maybe I just chose the right people.

I forced myself to throw the sheet back and then I sat up.

I really needed to get up and shower as the tenant next door was expecting me to come over at nine and fix some of the plumbing.

Yeah, I could have hired a plumber, but that would have cost money. Call me cheap—I prefer the term *frugal*—but I hated to spend money for professionals to come and do work that I was perfectly capable of doing. Oh, I'd call in electricians or plumbers for big jobs, but some household repairs were pretty minor things.

I headed into the bathroom and brushed my teeth.

The current tenant, George, was a nice-looking black fellow, from England. He wasn't very tall, but he had an athletic build, was always clean-looking, well-dressed, and had proven to be a delightful person to talk to. Not a thug-wannabe or pimp-rapper, but polite and well-spoken. He worked at a local warehouse, but had plans to move to Toronto soon with his girlfriend.

I had no idea if he knew that I was gay or not.

I wasn't blatant about my sexual preference—there were no rainbow flags flying from the porch, and no wild parties with half-naked men frolicking in the yard—but I didn't hide it either.

I enjoyed looking at men though and the sight of George's healthy-looking bulge in had inspired numerous fantasies over the last two years, even though I had always figured George for being quite straight.

Anyway, last night while I was doing my laundry, George had called and

asked if I could replace a leaking valve under his toilet. He'd been trying to manage the repair himself but had got things pretty screwed up. Now George is a very intelligent guy with a fantastic personality but just don't let him get his hands on a screwdriver or worse yet, a hammer. He had sounded pretty upset and was threatening to take some drastic steps with that toilet so I promised to come over first thing in the morning.

Well, now it was first thing and I wanted to get over there as quick as I could. All the jeans I usually wore for house-work were still in the wash, so I pulled on a raggedy old pair that I had saved for painting and yard work.

When I arrived, George was strutting around wearing only a pair of tight fitting bikini style underwear that made the shear bulk of his magnificent equipment quite evident. I couldn't keep my eyes off the healthy bulge under that tightly stretched fabric! He acted like he didn't notice but now I'm sure he must have. Right away he led me to the bathroom so I might survey the damage.

Well, that old pair of jeans I'd grabbed in my haste were way too tight for me and really should have been thrown away years ago. I could barely breath with the top snap closed, much less bend over. Before I could get down on all fours to look the situation over I had to pop the snap and rely on the zipper to keep my pants from falling down. I had thought to pull on any underwear that morning—I usually didn't bother when I was just planning on being around the house—so I was a bit concerned about that. Well, that damn zipper kept slipping down as I struggled to straighten out the piece of flexible copper tubing that connects the shut off valve to the toilet's tank. Before I realized it my jeans managed to get down far enough to expose the top of my crack.

It was about then that I noticed a change in George' mood and wondered what might of caused it. He had been pacing back and forth growling about plumbing in general then suddenly became very quite. I glanced back over my shoulder to see if he was even still in the bathroom and immediately noticed his bikini underwear looked considerably fuller than before.

"Can...can...I help you with that?" he asked nervously, as he suddenly knelt down behind me.

"Well..." I started to say *no,* but that was when I realized how far my jeans had worked themselves down and that it was the crack of my ass he was speaking to when he asked that question. I had to think fast. There was nothing in the world that I wanted more at that moment than to have him plough my little white ass with his big black cock but I had too great a fear that I had read the situation wrong. "You, ah, wouldn't happen to have any, ah, tubing like this around...would you?" I asked, speaking over my shoulder to his bulging dick. "Look how badly it's kinked here?"

George' swelling member was so close to my ass that I could feel the heat radiating from it! I pretended to struggle with the tubing for a moment to cover movements that brought my jeans down even further and allowed my bare butt to lightly bump against his rigid shaft.

"Where? I can't see..." George replied.

As he leaned forward to get a better look he sort of accidentally mashed his hard thick shaft into the crack of my now mostly bare ass. I could have cum right then!

"Uh...ah...right, ah...there." I stuttered then rolled my hips to drag my anus downward over his cotton-covered boner.

In response George leaned into me a bit more as he pretended to look where I was pointing then straightened up. I pivoted back with him to keep his shaft in my crack and did a couple of slow rolls with my hips to sort of jack him with my crevice. I didn't want to leave any doubt in his mind at this point as to what I wanted.

Then suddenly the wonderful contact of his thick hot shaft was gone!

At that moment I thought for sure I had fucked up big time. I could have cried! Then I looked over my shoulder and saw that he had stood and was pushing his bikini's down past his knees. And—oh my God!—his dick was longer, thicker and blacker than I had ever dreamed. It was absolutely beautiful! Nine or ten inches in length and almost two across. His shiny purple glans was longer than most and had an extended rake to it that I

instinctively new was going to help get his thick shaft up my ass.

As George knelt again I quickly kicked my jeans the rest of the way off. With my heart beating ninety miles an hour I stared down at the floor wondering if he was going to try to put it in without any lubrication. When I felt his broad tip press into my asshole I was relieved because it was wet with some spit that he had applied to it. He grasped my hips and his big plum of a tip began to force my entrance open. At that I started trembling all over. I pushed back against him as well until my over stretched anal ring began to hurt so bad that I had to lean forward again. George new what he was doing because he took it out then applied more spit to his dick then worked a wetted finger into my ass. Oh that felt great! I rolled my ass about on his digit to get my ring to stretch some and massage my prostate as

well.

"That better, Mason?" he asked softly as his broad tip went even deeper into me.

"Yeah! Much..." I said as I rotated my hips in a circular motion in an attempt to finally get his big black plum to go through.

Then in it went. And a bit too fast.

My sphincter was spasming painfully about his thick shaft but I wasn't about to

try to get away from him. My dream had come true! His beautiful black dick was actually in me and there was no way I was going to let it get away. Not just yet anyway. George could tell by the tension in my body that I was in discomfort though.

"Are you ok? Want me to take it out?"

"No! I exclaimed, glancing over my shoulder. "Good God no! Just give me a

second or two here ."

"Ok...no problem." George gave me a chuckle and a big grin.

I beat slowly at my meat as my anal ring stretched to adapt to his great girth. When I began pushing back he pushed in. His thick shaft sliding through the sensitive ring of nerves that lined my over stretched sphincter and the feeling of incredible fullness I was beginning to perceive almost set me off. Even though I had ceased beating my meat I almost went anyway when his broad glans seated itself against the top of my colon.

"Uh, that's about it. I don't think I can take anymore," I said with a nervous laugh. "How much is left??"

"Oh, about an inch."

Christ, I thought.

"You must have had some practice at this. The girlfriend's never been able to take this much." George began to slowly move in and out.

"Ah, yeah...I have." It felt *so good* in me. "Started in high school with classmates and kept going. It's been a while since I've had a good fucking though." Too long. "Lately though all I've taken back there is a dildo."

"Ah."

"It fills the need," I moaned, "but it's just not as good as the real thing. And

that's absolutely the biggest real thing that's ever been in there!" I said grinning as I looked over my shoulder at his big black pole undulating slowly between the cheeks of my skinny

white ass.

At that George increased his grip on my hips and began to really fuck me for all he was worth. He was trying to be careful to not over penetrate though. I did miss the sound and feel of hips slapping against my ass but the way his huge piston stirred my bowels more than made up for it. I wanted to wait for him but after a couple of strokes in row where he penetrated a little deeper than previously agreed upon I went off. And as you might expect, his plunges were not perceived as being anywhere near as pleasurable as before but I held on and waited for his release. Finally he went off, pumping gobs and gobs of sperm deeper into my bowels than ever it's ever been before.

"Shit man!" George gasped. "That was damn that was good! Are you up for an

instant replay?" His dick had lost some of it's girth and rigidity at that point and the slow short strokes he was giving me really did feel good. All that wonderful cum he had pumped in had added to the lubrication too.

"What the hell!" I replied with a big grin.

At that George shifted back to long full strokes again and my dick returned to full hard. George wasn't in such a hurry this time though and neither was I.

He must have fucked me for a good fifteen minutes or so before he went off for the second time. As soon as he did I slid off of him then spun around to take his still oozing dick in my mouth. Having his thick black glans mashed against the top of my mouth plus the taste of his sperm mixed with the bittersweet flavour of my ass brought me one of the

most intense ejaculations I've ever experienced in my entire life.

"Tell you what, Mason," George said afterwards with a wink and an affectionate squeeze to my rubbed raw and ever so red dick. "I'll pick up some tubing on my way home today and we can work on this some more tomorrow morning. I guess I can use the bathroom down in the basement for the meantime."

I nodded, still savouring the afterglow from the act.

"Just as well that Janine's not here this weekend," George continued. "She hates using the one in the basement. She's on the rag all this week anyway and she really gets cranky."

That explained why he was carrying such a big load. And speaking of that, my butt hole had been so well stretched that I couldn't get it to close all the way for nearly an hour.

Consequently, quite a bit of sperm leaked out of me as I walked home. I'm saving that old pair of jeans with his dried cum inside as a memento to that wonderful occasion.

Chapter Two

The following Friday, I was waiting for a technician to come over from Ma Bell.

George had left for Toronto for a long weekend with his girlfriend and so I had to be at home waiting to let the repairman in. I had better things I could be doing with my Friday morning, but what choice did I have? I couldn't fix the faulty phone jack myself—that was one of those home repairs when I did have to call in a professional—and the service call was scheduled for 'sometime between the hours of ten and two.

I guess I was stuck there until he showed...and then I could take off and run my errands.

Of course, Ma Bell's boys are rather known for never arriving in the time they say they will, so it was to my surprise, when a blue van drove up just a few minutes after noon.

I had been sitting in a chair and watching from the living room.

He was a good looking bloke. Probably a bit over thirty-five, six foot and with a buzz cut, or what I assumed was hair that had grown back after he'd gone for a skinhead. He wasn't particularly muscled under his work clothes, though he had nice arms, but he had a beautiful smile and a great bubble butt under his tight-fitting navy blue work pants.

"Hi there," he said as I opened the door. "I'm Craig, from *Bell*. What can I do for ya today?"

"Mason." I licked my lips. "The phone jack in the basement family room isn't working." I took Craig downstairs and showed him to the faulty phone jack, and he popped off the cover and instantly let out a grin.

"You been in this place long?"

"No, I don't actually live here. I own the whole building, but I rent out this half."

"Ah."

"The rest of the jacks work just fine, but George never bothered having a phone down here. He's got the one in the living room and the bedroom upstairs, so never bothered putting one in here. I think he's looking at buying a computer and he wants to hook up to the internet."

"Ah," the man repeated. "Well, whoever was here before tried to do some dodgy work on this. This is gonna take a while."

"All right. George will be happy for you to come back later and fix it then."

"Oh, there's no need for that." The technician grinned that beautiful grin at me again. "This is my last appointment for the day. I'm happy to stay here for as long as I need too."

"All right then." I leaned back and watched Craig set to work.

Craig chuckled. "It looks like your previous tenants tried to install a separate phone line down here, and they didn't want to have to pay for it. You can see here where they tried to link it off the currently faulty jack." He gestured with his finger. "This is a fairly easy fix, but it's quite fiddly. One wrong snip and you'll lose service for the whole place."

"That wouldn't be a good thing."

"Nope." Craig chuckled again.

I stood and watched while he fiddled around with different wires, unplugging some, reinstalling another. He had fixed everything, fairly quickly I thought, when he called out to me.

"Mason?"

"Yeah?"

"This is where it gets fiddly. Can you see the two wires I'm holding in place?"

"Yeah."

"Well I need to keep holding them in place while the faceplate gets screwed back into the wall. And I seem to have left my third arm back in the van. Do you reckon you can grab that screwdriver in my back pocket?"

I looked, and then took a second, longer look.

He was down on all fours, his work pants stretched tight over his beautiful ass, a Philip's head sticking out of the left pocket on his cheeks.

I licked my lips. Craig certainly wouldn't know I was gay. I had a deep voice and not an ounce of camp about me, but I couldn't help myself wanting to just have a bit of a feel. *I shouldn't do this,* I told myself. *But Christ, I want too!*

I tried to make it seem like part of the motion of getting the screwdriver—I slid my palm into his back pocket and gripped, and in the same motion took the screwdriver. I knew straight away it didn't go as smoothly as I'd hoped—I fumbled the grip. His ass was tight and fleshy under his pants, and even though I'd fucked up the discretion of copping a feel, I was glad for it.

Craig didn't seem to have noticed. "Okay, now come down here and screw in this faceplate, while I hold these two bastards in place."

I did as he told me. As I knelt beside him, I could smell his cologne, mixed in with his sweat. I wanted to drink it in. His skin was a Lochlyn bronzed tan, but not in a rough-trade kind of way, nor a fake-tan solarium kind of way. I suspect he probably has spent a lot of time at the beach over the summer.

I finished screwing in the plate and we stood up.

"So, do you always grab guys' asses?" he asked, with a blank expression on his face.

For all I knew he was about to punch me. I thought of excuses, and then realised that in the end, I'd been caught out. No lie would work. "Sorry. You've got a nice ass is all."

"I do," he nodded slowly, and then he flashed that grin again. "You should've asked."

I couldn't believe it—I was basically in a porn scene right now, down to the clumsy set-up of it all, but Craig was already unzipping his fly. He turned around and lowered his pants and his *Calvin Kleins* over his cheeks.

I quickly dropped onto my knees, and pushed his cheeks apart. I lowered my face down to his hole; he smelt manly—not sweaty or gross, just the general musk that builds up by lunchtime. His crack was deep, and it felt moist against my cheeks as I traced the outside of his hole with the tip of my tongue.

I felt him move away slightly as some guys do when you lick their hole. I put my hands on his groin and pulled him back into me. I flicked my tongue over his hole, and he moaned every time. I then started to go for broad strokes with my huge tongue. He moaned and shivered as I licked his sweet bud, and eventually, I pulled his cheeks apart and pushed my tongue up inside him.

He let out a long pleasurable groan, and shuddered. I reached around and felt for his cock, which had grown rock hard. I pulled it in time with the thrusts of my tongue into his hole, his balls slapping into my hand.

Craig moaned.

I stood up and pushed my own jeans down to my ankles. My cock was as hard as granite. I ran the head up the length of his crack, letting it slide along with the spit I'd left there.

"Yeah, fuck me man!" he grunted.

I leaned forward and put two fingers his mouth. He slurped them up eagerly. I flattened my cock down into his crack and pushed against him, teasing him. With my free hand, I reached forward, under his shirt and started tweaking his nipples. He bit down gently on my fingers, and I pushed his jaw shut harder around them. I liked the pain.

I pushed the head of my cock into his warm, wet, tight hole, and he groaned around my fingers, which he was still biting and sucking. I pulled the head out, and did it again. More groans. I took my spit-covered fingers out form his mouth, and he started panting, his voice rising in pitch "Fuck me! Fuck me fuck me! Please - fuck me!" I took my head out again and slid my fingers into his hole, spinning them round, pulling on his prostate, driving him wild.

I replaced my fingers with my cock head, only this time, I drove the entire shaft up his arse in one motion. He went silent for a moment as he dealt with the pain. Then I started pumping. By this time we were flat on the rec room's floor, and I got up on my elbows, and my knees, and drove my cock into him as fast and hard as I could. He was moaning with each thrust, and though I'm sure it hurt him, he loved it, and I loved feeling my cock in his arse.

"Oh God!" I gasped as I came, five huge squirts into his crack, and then I slowly stopped thrusting. I was still hard, and could've kept going.

His voice was shaky, still coping with my cock in his arse. "Bugger...I wanted to swallow it."

I whipped my cock out of his hole and sucked as much of my cum out of his arse as I could. I jacked his cock at the same time, and when I felt it tighten, I flipped him over so he could shoot on his stomach. With my load still in my mouth, I scooped his cum off his chest and belly, then let my tongue hang over his mouth and all our jizz flow forth into his waiting throat.

Then we made out, the taste of cum and arse still on my tongue, before he decided it was time to leave. While he was pulling his pants up, I smacked his ass once, and then, with an oddly tender hug, he left.

Ever since, I've been hoping for my phone to fuck up so I might have him called out to my home.

Chapter Three

Monday morning saw me back at work. Since I'd started working as a delivery person for a furniture store, I had become rather familiar with driving the city streets. Prior to that I knew the basics, but little more, since I grew up in a smaller town just outside the city. The daily commute hadn't been more than about fifteen minutes, which was tolerable, but I had saved up enough for a down payment on a house, deciding to buy a duplex so that I would have the rental income to help pay the bills.

Anyway, the driving around was fairly easy. It gave me some good experience, in the unlikely case I wanted to follow one of my many silly, on-the-fly impulses, namely the recurring impulse to become a taxi driver.

Even though I had the indispensable help of mechanical conveniences, moving furniture around also helped keep me in relatively good shape. It was sort of a blessing, since although I liked a good day of physical labour, I would never otherwise work out—well, no in a gym, anyways.

I always drove a cube van, just a delivery truck like couriers use, and I usually drove alone. I sort of liked the solitude, just to contemplate the many things that my mind loved to play mental acrobatics with. I always kept my mind on the road, but it still gave me an opportunity to spend some quiet time alone. Occasionally I even liked to have someone along for company, but for the most part I enjoyed having some time to myself.

I'd arrived for work in the morning, as usual, and walked through the back entrance. The store was fairly large, one of the biggest in the area, with a huge warehouse area in addition to the showroom. I skirted the warehouse area—no need to go there yet—and I never went on the sales floor. Like I said, the place was big and busy—a hundred regular staff, at least, along with some fresh seasonal employees just starting—with everyone scattered between the various departments.

I nodded to a few of my closer acquaintances. With the number of staff, I often passed a lot of people in the halls that I've not seen or had no connection with.

There's this one guy I've seen a handful of times in passing, usually when he's going to the water cooler to top up his bottle. He's tall, lean, pale and dark-haired...just my type if he was gay! He has lovely high cheek bones and usually a little flush with cute red cheeks and he has lovely deep blue eyes and long eye lashes. He was one of the salesmen, who worked out in the showroom.

On a few days, our trips to the water cooler or coffee machine have coincided and I've always given him a friendly smile as I eyed him up but this one particular day it seemed that every single time I went, he was there, and then my trips to the bathroom were in time with his too! Whenever I went to take a piss he'd either just be coming out or just going in when I came out.

There were no deliveries for that day, so I was at my small desk working to try and get caught up on paperwork. Instead of working though, I kept imagining taking a piss next to him and checking out his cock. I really hoped I'd get a chance! I even started to take trips to the toilet even when I didn't need it just to try and bump into him.

After about the fourth time I had a close call, but was just zipping up when he came in so missed it. I couldn't very well flop my cock and balls back out and return to the urinal when it was obvious I had just finished. I missed my chance!

Finally at five o'clock I went one last time to take a genuine piss. I always take my cock and balls out completely when I go for a piss—it's nice to let my big package have a little freedom for a minute or two. So there I was taking a wiz, my balls hanging nicely out my jeans and to my delight the hot cooler guy takes the urinal one over from mine. I shifted and turned towards him moving my arm on his side out of the way so if he wanted he could get a look at my cock and low hanging smooth balls. I was pissing like a race horse, my foreskin pulled back slightly so I didn't make a shower everywhere but had one nice clean stream of piss. I looked over to get a glimpse of what he had but from my angle his arm was in the way so I couldn't see. Looking up I saw he was blatantly checking out my cock, so as my piss stream slowed I gave it a shake for him. He looked up and saw me watching him watching my cock, embarrassed he looked away. I turned towards him more so he could get an even better look and rolled my foreskin back and forth, as if shaking out the last little drips. He looked back and saw me playing with it, then looked me in the eye. I gave him a cheeky grin and nodded my head towards his own exposed cock. He took the hint and shifted so I could get a look. He had a beautiful long, perfectly straight, thin uncut cock, which was almost completely rock hard. Looking at it I couldn't help lick my lips.

I looked him in the eye, gave him a wink and then without even tucking myself away I turned and went into the disabled cubicle, pushing the door behind me without locking it.

Seconds felt like hours but finally he took the bait and gingerly followed me in.

I locked the door behind him and took his uncut cock in my hand. It was long, thin and soon rock hard! It must have been a good eight and half, even nine inches.

I grabbed his hand and moved it my cock and soon we had each other's hard meat in our hands rubbing up and down. His foreskin slid back over his large mushroom head revealing a nice purple bell end and slit oozing pre cum. I sat on the toilet lid, undid his trousers top button and let his pants drop to the floor. I licked the pre cum of his head and then started teasing it with the tip of my tongue. Then I took his cock head in my mouth and sucked it hard. I reached round and grabbed his firm smooth small butt cheeks pushing his hips in towards me so his shaft slid down my throat. I managed about half of it before I started to gag. I sucked up and down his shaft a while, he was now really hard and his low hanging balls were swinging below my chin.

I stood up and unbuttoned his shirt.

The hot salesman was now stood naked in front of me, in just his smart work shoes and socks. It was great! With my hand on his shoulder I gently encouraged him down onto his knees where he eagerly devoured my cock. No gentle build up, no teasing me with his tongue, he took the whole of my thick eight inch tool down his throat and sucked it like a pro. I hadn't had my cock deep throated like that in a long while and I fucking loved it!

I soon had my hands on the back of his head and was fucking his face for all it's worth and he could handle every inch with ease! As much as I loved it I didn't want to cum just yet. I slid my cock out and got him to stand back up.

My turn on my knees I did my best to deep throat his cock but couldn't manage it.

"Rim me," he ordered as he pulled out. He turned around and bent over leaning on the disabled hand rail thing by the mirror. From this angle I had perfect access to his tight pucker hole. He had a small amount of soft dark hair round the rim and smooth, pail, rock hard, perfectly formed small bubble butt. I got to work flicking my tongue across his hole and then burying it deep inside. From this angle I could see, in the mirror, his big rock hard cock and low hanging balls swinging around. He started to moan with pleasure but I didn't even care about the noise, this was too fun! As well as rimming him I started to finger him until I had three fingers buried deep inside him.

"Fuck me," he whispered, quietly between moans.

He didn't have to ask twice. I stood up and positioned my bulging cock head at his tight hole. Pushing forward his pucker parted quite easily and my helmet disappeared inside him. I slid my cock half in, but about half way is where I get really thick and he tensed up and pulled away from me a bit. I pulled back sliding my cock back out till just my head remained, and then slid it back down inside to thickest part again. I repeated this motion until his ass had adjusted to my girth and soon I was buried up to my light furry pubes and ball sack. I pulled out again and thrust in deeper and harder. Now I had my rhythm I was fucking him hard and deep.

But not hard enough for him, he reached round and grab my leg pulling me deeper into him. I braced against the hand rail and I ploughed into him with all my might. He moaned, in pleasure I think and I repeated the process.

Our grunts were getting so loud that he had to pick up his tie and bite down on it! After several more thrusts he let out a long loud moan and shot his load all over the floor and mirror. This made his ass muscle contract round my throbbing cock and set me off; so that I shot a big juicy load deep inside his ass. The force of my eruption set him off again and he shot a few more times on the floor.

My cock slid out of him and I stumbled back coming to a rest sitting on the toilet seat again.

He turned round his cock still impressively hard and then slumped to the cold tile floor next to me.

At this point it occurred to me I didn't even know his name! "I'm Mason," I said, offering my hand. "Nice to meet you."

"William," he replied reaching up his hand to shake mine. I pulled him up and he straddled my lap, our wet juicy cocks sliding against each others as they softened.

We embraced for a while and soon my cock perked up again.

When William felt my hard cock pushing against his, he looked down and said, "Hello? What's this?" and then he dropped to his knees in front of me. With him deep-throating my cock again, it didn't take long for me to shoot a hot wad down his throat. He stood up, licking his lips, and his long perfectly straight cock was at my own lips.

I instinctively opened wide and took as much down my throat as I could. I tried my best to deep-throat it again but I still wasn't getting all of him in, but William seemed to enjoy me face-fucking him even so.

After a while of his balls slapping my chin and cock making me gag he pulled out and shook his head. "I won't cum again today."

"Tomorrow?" I asked with a wink.

"Yeah, tomorrow it is." William hastily snatched up his pants and we both hastily got dressed.

I slipped out of the disabled cubicle, leaving him to discreetly slip out after I was gone...

No one had noticed our absence.

After closing, I was still hard and horny. William had vanished before I could stop and invite him back to my place.

I swung by one of the local bars—the one known to have a gay clientele. The city was too small and provincial to support its own gay bar, but we knew where we could hang out...as long as we weren't too blatant.

I pulled into the parking lot and undid a few buttons on my shirt, to better show off my hairy chest.

I walked into the bar and looked around. I didn't see anyone I knew. Damn.

I bought a beer and slumped onto one of the barstools.

"I'll have whatever's on tap," a deep baritone announced.

I turned my head around.

He was about five ten, with a medium build, dark hair, brown eyes, and was simply bloody stunning. He is looked like his in his mid-twenties. Then he smiled at me.

He had the cutest smile!

"Is this seat taken?"

"Nope." I shook my head and watched him sit down.

We chatted for a bit.

Jon was thirty-two, but he could pass for twenty-five. He was in-town on business.

As the night went on, I was getting more and more horny with the prospect of wanting to have a little fun with him. He didn't seem to be offended by my constantly staring at him, and he was checking me out equally.

Finally, I finished my drink. "Can I offer you a ride home?" I asked.

"Sure. I'm staying with family on this trip."

We didn't speak much as we drove towards his place. I wanted to ask him if he fancied going for a drive somewhere, but couldn't. So, when I pulled into the parking lot, I just blurted out and asked him.

Jon looked somewhat startled and taken aback by the question, but then he nodded. "Sure."

"Fantastic!" I was giving him the grand tour while we drove around. We spoke for a little about this and that, before the urge to have some sort of contact took hold.

Jon reached over and started stroking my leg. "We could head back to your place," he said, "and have ourselves some fun."

"Yeah." I was rock-hard now and really straining my jeans.

Jon's own pants were bulging as well.

"Fuck, I can't wait that long." We were on the wrong side of town, as far away from my place as we could get. But, inspiration struck and I headed for a deserted track I knew, just on the outskirts of town.

It was pissing it down. Really heavy at times, but it wasn't really that cold. That nice summer rain. We pulled into a dirt track, one I know would be safe, and I turned the lights and engine off.

Jon frowned. "You leave out here?"

"No, but this place is private." I leaned over to him and kissed him, lightly at first, then gave it all I could. He tasted so good, and was an expert kisser. I couldn't hold myself back, and started to caress his body touching every part of him. He had a tight body, with a light speckling of hair on his chest. His train of hair to below his waist line was like perfection! I continued to explore his mouth with my tongue, and his body with my hands!

In an effort to allow us more access, we dropped the seats right back to near horizontal. He lay on top of me, embraced in a passionate kiss, and still caressing each other. I felt his arse and back, pulling him ever closer to me. Then we swapped positions, I lay on him, running my now hardened cock against his groin...it was heaven, the rain thumping down around us, and two lads, locked together!

I couldn't resist it any longer, I had to expose him. I went down to his waist line, and undid his belt, then his buttons. His rock hard cock was straining to be released, and I was happy to oblige. I played with his pants, and felt its hardness. I rubbed it, while still kissing him.

We had to get naked, so we removed each other's clothing. We were both naked, and within seconds were locked into each other's embrace again. I went on to kiss him all over, his neck, his check, his tummy, working my way down to his waist line. His hard cock standing proud below my chin, I decided to go the long way around. I moved to his left hip, kissing and licking as I went down, moving down to his legs, and then to his balls! To my delight, he was shaved. His huge sack hung down low, shaven and tasting and feeling amazing. I wasted no time in licking and sucking him, making him moan. His balls were warm and so inviting!

Then, his cock! Standing thick set and seven inches, it rose towards his belly button! I worked at the base, licking and sucking, before moving up his thick shaft, nibbling as I went. The, I reached the head. He is uncut, and was already leaking pre-cum. I decided to take the full length all the way down to its based, rubbing my tongue as I went down. I felt so good as it slid down my throat. Then, I buried my nose in his balls as I sucked like I hadn't sucked before! He moaned as I worked his thick cock!

Then, he flipped me over onto my back, and he straddled me. His warm body against mine was truly amazing, and he pinned me down and kissed me. His thrusts against me were rubbing my already rock hard cock! He moved down to my cock and took it expertly into his mouth and bobbed his head up and down. It felt amazing having his warm mouth around my hard cock. His tongue swirled around my cock. I felt like a needed to blow a load! But I held myself back. He moved back up to continue kissing me, but this timed pushed my legs up and around his waist. His cock was rubbing around my ball sack and the top of my leg, and I shuffled around a bit to allow his cock access to my arse. The rain continued to beat down on the car roof!

I couldn't hold it anymore and wanted him to fuck me. So, I flipped him onto his back, and massaged his cock. I usually keep condom and lube packs in my car, just in case, so a leant over and took one out. I took the condom out and slowly put it over his cock and guided it down his thick cock. Then, I massaged lube into his hard cock and also my arse. I wanted to control the start of this, so decided to get on top of him, and slide down his cock to start with. This way I could control his thick cock and the speed! I slide down, which looking into his eyes and squeezed my arse muscle, so that he felt it. He was moaning as he looked into mine.

As I got used to his cock, I reached down to mine and slowly started to stroke, using the left over lube. I bobbed up and down his thick shaft, in the limited space of my car. It felt so good. We kissed, and he also started to thrust up into me.

The rain started to ease a little, so I suggested we take this outside. He was reluctant at first, but I persuaded him to come outside with me (it helps that as I spoke I was still bobbing up and down on his hard cock).

He maneuvered out of the car, and stood up in the light rain. It wasn't raining too hard, and it was so warm. I was so hot to be outside, naked, and with a hot sexy guy. I positioned myself up against my car, so he was behind me. I bent down slightly, and allowed him to slide his cock into me. He put one hand on my shoulder, and one on my waist, and he started to pump. He started slow at first, delicate, then went all out and fucked me hard up against my car. I was stroking my hardened cock as he filled my arse with his meat.

After a short time, he got close, and came hard into the condom! The rain was beating down on us both as he moaned as he shot his load deep into the condom!

I stood up, with him still inside, and turned my head around for a kiss. It was like ecstasy! He slowly went soft inside me and also pulled out, still panting from hard fucking me up against the car.

We got back into the car, and had a further kiss and a cuddle before I drove him home.

Chapter Four

It was a month or so after that adventure with William and Jon that I met up with Kurt, the satellite man. Satellite boy is more accurate, because that's what he looked like. In all his twenty-four years, he still looked like he was sixteen or seventeen years old. He was about five foot five, one thirty, with a short tight body. He was nicely compact. His short clipped blond hair and barely a wisp of peach-fuzz on his upper lip, made him look very young. So young, I would have, had I known better, dismissed him as jail-bait.

But, this was no boy. Underneath his *Levi's* and tight tee-shirt, he was all man. The kind of body that looks naturally built, not from hours in a gym, but hours of hard work. Slightly developed pecs, and nipples that were as big around as a dime and tips that stretched his shirt from his body.

He was completely smooth from the waist up, not even the hint of fur on his smooth skin. And below the belt, a small bush of true blond hair, crowing a beautifully shaped cock. Flaccid, his dick curved down and hung a good 5 inches. Resting on a pair of walnut sized balls. His dick did rest on them, truly regally. Well developed thighs and calves. A butt that you'd expect to see on a sculpture in a museum, firm and totally smooth. Covering his legs, a moderate pelt of soft fur. Yep, this was a beautiful boy, the kind you wouldn't take home to mother, afraid she'd scoop him up. But I'm proceeding myself.

Kurt worked as a service rep for a local satellite company, and seemed to do very good for himself.

As it be, I was having his company install service to my half of the duplex...after not bothering with cable for years, it was finally time to splurge.

Kurt would have to make an initial visit to take care of the paperwork and schedule the actual installation.

Now I didn't flaunt my sexual orientation too much. The living room and so-called public areas of my home were fairly safe, but in my bedroom I went all out. One glance in there and it was obvious to anyone educated that I was gay. The large rainbow flag and pictures of men in white briefs, a particular fetish, adorning the walls, was a pretty clear signal.

Upon Kurt's visit, we discussed the hardware that would need to be installed and location. I showed him the living room and then down into the basement rec room where I actually wanted the main television to be set up.

"And I was thinking about having the set in my room as well."

"Yeah, you'll need a second receiver for that." Kurt was making notes in a small notebook. He looked around at my bedroom—did his gaze linger on those pictures for longer than casual interest?—and then we returned to the living room.

Through the entire meeting, I noticed that Kurt kept fidgeting in his seat. Occasionally I would catch him glancing down the hallway to the pictures on my bedroom wall. After all the business was done, we sat and idly chit chat.

"Would you like something to drink?"

"Juice would be fine. Thanks."

As I arose to go to the kitchen, I finally found out why he was so fidgety.

I noticed his dick slowly growing down his left leg. He looked uncomfortable, trying to work his dick down his pant leg, it kept growing. By the time I'd returned with his drink, the thing snaked down his leg about eight inches, and was growing plumper.

"So," I said, "that looks uncomfortable trapped in your pants." I pointed to his hard-on.

"Yeah, it's getting that way," Kurt replied with a sheepish grin. He was blushing too.

"So why don't you take your pants off and get comfortable," I asked him.

"I've only done this a few times." Kurt spoke quietly and shyly.

I smiled back at him. "That's okay, just enjoy the feelings." I had the chance to give this boy so many new pleasures.

As he undid his belt and pulled open his jeans, I saw the waistband of his white briefs. He stopped short of pulling his pants down to bend over and untie his work boots. As he bent over, I could see his beautiful butt stretch the rear of his jeans.

After kicking off his boots, he finished removed his jeans, pulling them slowly down his thighs. They were obviously very form-fitting. A beautifully formed cock hung out of the left leg of his briefs. He gingerly reached through his briefs and pulled his dick back into his underwear, making a sizable pouch in the front. Kurt looked at me and blushed again. "I usually don't wear briefs, but boxers instead, they aren't as confining."

"I'm not complaining." And they were confining—the pouch stretched his briefs tightly across his thighs.

He unbuttoned his shirt, revealing a beautiful chest.

I quickly shucked off own my tee-shirt and sweats, leaving my briefs on. I was too quickly tenting out my briefs. "Would you like to go into the bedroom?" I asked him.

"Sure," he replied.

I laid him down on the bed and stepped back to admire his beautifully boyish body. Just the sight of this boy, made my dick jump in my briefs.

I wanted to taste every inch of his body. I sat to the side of the bed and nuzzled my head to the pouch in his underwear. The material stretched even more. I slowly licked around the waistband of his underwear, to his naval. This sent shivers through the boy. I worked my tongue down, over his smooth belly to his crotch. I savoured the sweet smell of the boy.

I placed my mouth over his crotch, sucking his dick through the material. I lightly bit at his dick, making the material wet. I made my way down his pouch, to the underside of his briefs. Licking the leg band and his leg, I again took a deep breath of the sweetness. I placed my head firmly between his legs and licked at the material covering his ass.

Kurt's body shook, as I nipped at his hole.

I could hardly control myself as his softly furred legs closed around my head, and his butt clinched my tongue at his hole. This boy had the tastiest body and I wanted more.

I pulled myself up, my body on top of his. I took my head to his lips and playfully nipped at his lower lip. He instantly opened his mouth and sucked my upper lip into his mouth. I responded by licking my tongue across his lower teeth. He plunged his tongue deep into my mouth licking, and sucking my tongue into him. His lips were soft as he nipped at my tongue with them.

I slipped my tongue out of his mouth, to lick his jaw line to his ears. I nipped at his ear lobe, taking it into my mouth. Again he shivered with pleasure. I worked my tongue back down his neck, following the underside of his jaw. I sucked and licked his neck playfully, not to bruise his smooth skin. I worked my mouth up the other side to his other ear. And again sucked the lobe into my mouth.

These seemed to be pleasure points on this boy, because he moaned, gasped and shivered down his body. This seemed to be turning the boy on, as I noticed his nipples growing firmer. I moved my mouth down his neck to his chest. I took his left nipple into my mouth and bit lightly, teasing the tip with my tongue. I swirled my tongue around his nipple, he replied with a great moan and sigh. I had this boy turned on and loving every minute of it.

I worked my way across his chest to his other nipple, again playfully nipping it with my teeth. He reached up and grasped my head holding me tightly to his chest. I responded by sucking his nipple a little harder and nipping more at it.

I licked my way up the line of his pectoral muscle to his right arm pit. I gently lifted his arm to expose a beautiful, small patch of hair. I inhaled deeply, savouring the sweet smell. I worked my tongue across the patch, tugging at the hair. Kurt giggled and pulled away slightly, my touch was light and I guess it tickled him.

I dove back in, this time with a firmer sucking, and he moaned with pleasure. I licked my tongue over the entire area, again breathing deeply. I dragged my tongue across his chest, to his left pit and licked it completely. The boy had obviously never had a man lick his body so sweetly, he shuddered at my touch.

I lowered myself back down to his crotch. The pouch was stretched to its limits, with his dick screaming for release. I licked around the top of the waist band of his briefs, teasing his smooth belly with my tongue.

I took the waist band in my teeth and pulled down just far enough to reveal the head of his dick. Letting the band hold his dick in place, I licked at only his head. I took only the head into my mouth, and it swelled just a little bit more. I swirled my tongue around the cut head, paying special attention to the ridge just below the crown of his dick. I took the very tip and teased my tongue at the slit of the head. I could taste the bitter sweet pre-cum as just a drop formed and worked its way up. Using my tongue, I spread the drop over the head of his dick, covering his whole head with the taste of the boys pre-cum.

I pulled his briefs down to where they cradled his balls. His cock, as fully rigid as it could possibly be, stretched across his bush and over his belly, just covering his naval. His cock was about a good nine inches in length and six or more around. It was very smooth, stiff and with no sign of any wrinkling of the skin. It was like white marble. A perfect example of circumcision done right. Just one velvet cylinder of flesh.

I couldn't resist the urge to swallow his cock, all the way down my throat. Instead, I slowly took it into my mouth. Going down only far enough fill my mouth, I swirled my tongue around his member. Lightly sucking and licking it like a big straw. Kurt threw his head back as far into the pillow with a moan, his hips trying to thrust more of his dick into my mouth.

I felt as the head probed at my throat. Inhaling deeply, I let him thrust his dick deep into my throat. I fought to control my gag reflex and let his cock slip deeper into me. I could feel his pubic hairs on my upper lip, as I grounded his cock into me.

He moaned out loud. "I've never had my dick this deep into a mans throat!" He

was now thrashing in ecstasy. I worked my throat around his dick by trying to use my swallowing muscles in my neck. I was milking his cock with my throat.

I slowly withdrew his dick out of my throat, stopping only suck and nip at the head. His dick was beautiful, covered in saliva, it glistened in the light.

I slowly took his dick all the way back down into my throat. I reached up and rubbed his pecs with my palms, dragging them across his rigid nipples. I pinched them lightly between my fingers. The combined playing with his nipples and my throat milking his dick, made the boy groan loudly.

His hips thrusting forward, trying to get deeper into my throat. I let his dick slide out of my mouth, licking the shaft down to his balls. His sac was naturally hairless, I'd never seen a post-pubescent boy so clean of hair. His balls hung nicely, with its two nicely sized

testicles. I opened my mouth widely, almost not wide enough to get both nuts into my mouth. With a light suction, I was able to suck them past my fully stretched lips. He grunted lightly as they slipped into my mouth. Making my lips a snug ring around his balls. I felt his balls push further into my mouth and relax, filling my entire mouth.

As much as I could, without hurting his balls, I swirled my tongue around the sensitive flesh His cock throbbed and bounced against his belly wildly.

I pulled my head back and his sac pulled out of my mouth with plop from suction. He pulled my head up to his and kissed me deeply. He was darting his tongue around my mouth, tasting every inch.

"I'm not very experienced, but can I suck on your cock?" he asked in a whisper.

I had forgotten entirely about my own dick, just enjoying tasting this boy. "Sure," I replied. "Go slow and give it your best try." My own dick was stretching my briefs. I've got about eight inches and kinda thick, with a wicked curve to the left. Just enough to slide down a talented throat comfortably.

He lowered himself to my crotch. Staring intently at the throbbing pouch, he seemed unsure of himself.

"Just start licking it," I told him. "Take it slow." I was being given the pleasure of teaching this boy the joys of sucking dick.

Slipping my thumbs into the waistband of my briefs, I pulled them down and off. The boy took my dick into his mouth and tried to swallow the whole thing at once, gagging on is length. He was new to sucking dick, but had the potential to learn to give one hell of a blowjob. His mouth was smooth as silk, his tongue seemed to know just how to dart around my cock. He then only took the head of my dick, moving his tongue around the head and caressing the crown, like I had done his.

He removed his mouth from my dick. "Am I doing it right?"

All I could do was moan, this boy was making my dick feel so good. "Boy, you are doing great, just take it slowly."

He replaced his mouth over my dick, taking a little more, stroking my dick with his lips. He figured out that if taken from one side, my dick could slide in comfortably into and down his throat without much resistance. The next thing I realized, was that he had my dick planted firmly in his throat. All eight inches in him. As he pulled up I could see the smile on his face, from learning how to throat a dick.

Once he got used to my dick sliding in and out of his throat, he was bobbing up and down more swiftly. He seemed to take great pleasure in learning to throat a dick. I could feel my balls pulling tighter up into my body, signalling that I was ready to cum, I quickly pulled his mouth off my dick, I didn't want to cum just yet.

He took his lessons well, he lifted himself up to my chest and took a nipple in his mouth. He sucked and bit a little hard, which made me wince.

Kurt looked up, upset. "Did I hurt you?"

"Not at all boy, I enjoy rough play with my nipples."

He took my cue and placed his mouth on my nipple and sucked harder, little more than lightly nipping at the nipple. He sucked it in as hard as he could, then firmly bit the tip and worked his tongue across it.

This boy was good and learned well. He moved to the other nipple and gave it the same treatment, teasing me into ecstasy.

I lifted his head to mine. "Have you ever fucked a man or been fucked?"

"I've fucked a man before, but I've never been fucked."

"So, can I fuck you?"

"Well..." he replied a little hesitantly, "will it hurt?"

"It might at first, but I'll go slow and if you're too uncomfortable, I will stop."

"Promise?"

"Of course."

"Okay then," he replied.

I lifted his legs back and he instinctively grabbed his legs around the knees with his arms. Exposed was the prettiest smooth hole I had even seen. Totally hairless with a soft pink ring. I lowered my head a licked his butt avoiding his hole. He was thrusting his butt towards my tongue. I licked the firm cheeks around his hole. Then one lick across his hole and the boy spasmed with pleasure. I continued to tease at his hole with my tongue. The boy relaxed until I placed my tongue firmly against his hole and started to dart my tongue into his hole. He was squealing with delight as I stuck my tongue as deep as his tight hole would allow, his hips bucking back to my tongue. I felt his hole relaxing, feeling that he could take me slowly, I reached for the lube. The thick slippery kind, this boy was going to need all the help he could get. I applied a large coating of lube to his hole. Slowly pushing one finger than two, he winced. I know that I was going to have to go easy on this boy, not my normal thrashing.

I lubed up my dick—by now it was throbbing so much it almost hurt, begging for release. I placed the head to the boy's hole, he looked up at me with a look of pleading.

"Please, go easy on me," he begged.

Such was his look of desire but fear also. "I will, just try to relax and breath deeply, I will go slowly." I pushed just the head into his butt, feeling his hole squeeze tightly

around my dick. The boy bit into his lower lip, trying to relax and allow his hole to open up. He gripped my thighs tightly in response to the pain. I held it just inside him allowing his hole to stop spasming.

Seeing a relaxed look come over his face, I pushed a little deeper into his hole. He was not relaxing, and I could feel his spasming tighter around my dick. I could feel his butt trying to push out the invading object. "Just breath deeply and try not to push."

After a few deep breaths, his body seemed to release its tension, and relax. Then I could feel him pushing his hole slowly back onto my dick. This boy was hot for it and wanted more of me in him. I had gotten about six inches into him before he again tensed up and let out a gasp. I stopped where I was to let him get used to the size.

"That's good boy," I whispered into his ear. "I'll take it slow." But then in one swift move Kurt bucked his ass back onto my dick, taking it all the way to my balls. He gasped loudly.

"Oh god, please hold it there, don't pull out." He was almost sobbing through the pain. "Oh god, it hurts!"

"I'll pull out."

"No," he begged.

I held my dick in him until I could feel his hole stop squeezing hard. I began to slowly grind my crotch against his hole, stirring my dick in his ass. The boy kept bucking back to get more. I slowly started to withdraw my dick only to half way and then pushed it back in. He was quickly growing used to the intrusion in his ass. I started to pull a little further out with each stroke.

Abruptly, Kurt had a grin of sheer delight as I quickened my pace, pulling out

almost to the head and shoving it back in. Soon he was begging for it. "Oh god, please fuck me, please fuck me harder!"

So I gave him what he wanted. I love to hear a man beg me to plough his ass. I was pistoning my dick in and out of him at a furious pace. Again, I felt the oncoming feelings of orgasm, and I slowly pulled. He looked to me with a puzzled frown. I gave him a smile. "I'm too close and not ready to cum."

"Oh."

"Anyway, I want you to fuck me now," I said. I rolled over onto my back and lifted my legs. I grabbed a handful of lube and applied it generously to my hole. Inserting one finger then two then a third. I reached around with my other hand and proceeded to insert

another finger, massaging and pulling my hole open. Kurt seemed to enjoy watching me play with my hole. He stared in amazement at how my hole opened up.

While having had my share of dicks up my ass, this boy was still quite large. I've had fantasies of, but still never found that all glorious thirteen inches we so often hear about.

Kurt carefully positioned himself in front of my ass. I lubed him up quite generously. With some apprehension, he placed the head of his dick at my hole.

"It's okay, boy, go ahead and push it in."

"But I don't want to hurt you."

"You're not going to hurt me any more than I want to," I replied. I felt the head of his dick slowly slide into my ass. Without stopping, he planted his whole dick, all nine glorious inches of it, in up to his balls. I gasped at the size, oh yeah it hurt, but it hurt good. Now *this* was something the boy was experienced at.

He pulled his entire dick out and plunged it back into my ass, with an accuracy unmatched. He continued to pull his dick all the way out and back in several times. Then he would ground his dick into my hole, trying to get further into my ass.

"God," he moaned. "No one has ever been able to take me like this!"

Boy, you need some better playmates, I thought. How could anybody deny the

pleasures this boy had to offer?

Kurt continued to fuck my ass for a while without ever getting close to cumming or going soft. Ah, the blessings of youth. I reached for the lube and started stroking my neglected cock. Each time Kurt would pull all the way out and back, he would hit that spot on the prostrate, and force a little cum out my dick. Just the sight of this boy's body and the fucking he was throwing into me was making my mind reel. Then the all too familiar constriction of my nuts signalled that I was going to shoot.

And shoot I did! The first stream hit me square in the face. I convulsed uncontrollably as this boy pumped my cum out of my prostrate and across my body. A least seven streams later, I felt Kurt rip his dick from my ass and start stroking his own cock feverishly. As only a boy can, he shot his cum, hitting my face. I widely opened my mouth to catch what ever cum could make it to my mouth. A good five globs of cum was caught in my mouth, and the rest decorated my chest and belly.

Kurt collapsed forward on top of me. We rubbed the cum between us, sliding back and forth. Our mouths met in a deep kiss. We were both trying feverishly taste each other's mouths. Kurt then licked the cum running down my chin and face. He wanted to taste his own cum, then licked at my cum-laden chest. He put his mouth back over so that I could taste our cum mixed together, it was sweet as only a young man's cum is.

We lay there exhausted for a while.

Finally I turned my head to look at him. "Do you want to jump into the shower and get cleaned up?" I asked.

"No way," Kurt replied. "I want to feel and smell our cum on my body all day long." He was grinning widely now.

Chapter Five

George had given his notice. He and his girlfriend, Janine, were moving to Toronto and now I had to find another tenant to rent the place.

I thought back to the first year I had bought the house. I'd bought it in the fall and quite enjoyed the last bit of yard work. Then the snow came. We were supposedly in for a heavy winter and those come with a lot of shovelling.

The first big fall of the year was a heavy one, starting in mid-afternoon and continuing on into the night. At times the falling snow had been so thick that I couldn't see across the street.

It had finally stopped snowing around two a.m., and seeing as I was still wide awake, I decided to go out and work off some energy. About two weeks before, I'd rented the other half of the duplex to this guy who was about twenty-seven. We had hardly spoken, other than to show him the house and then sign the papers. He worked odd shifts, and so we usually just missed running into each other. Which was a real damn shame as he was quite gorgeous and the very first time I'd met him, I had wanted to rip his clothes off and see what was underneath.

Alex was six foot, one-seventy, with dark blonde hair, green/blue eyes, and just a bit of tan. He was a mix of cute and sexy.

Anyway, that night I'd gotten all geared up and went outside to start shovelling and found Alex had just come home from work and decided to help clear the snow away.

"You don't have to do this," I told him.

"Well, Mason, I do live here too." He gave me a smile, standing in the snow. "Crazy weather isn't it? It came down so fast!"

"I hope the rest of the winter isn't like this," I replied. We both made small talk while we continued shovelling. About twenty minutes into it, I had to get a drink, and so I left Alex still shovelling the driveway. I went inside and grabbed two bottles of water from the fridge.

When I got back out, Alex had abandoned the shovel and was just reaching for the door into his place. "Do you want some water?" I asked.

"Thanks." He turned and trudged through the snow towards me. "I was just on my way in to grab one."

So we took a quick break and talked a bit more, before picking up our shovels again.

"At least with the two of us, we'll get it done tonight."

"Yep." So we kept working. The poor man had no idea just how attracted towards him that I was feeling, and I was continually checking him out while we cleared the snow off the driveway. His jeans were stretched tight across his ass and his broad shoulders strained at his leather bomber jacket.

We were finally done, having shovelled our way down to the road. There was no sign of the ploughs being out yet though.

"They never show up until after you're done and gone back inside," Alex said. "Then they come along and fill your driveway back in."

"Yeah," I nodded. "I hate that."

"So, do you want to pop in for a bit?" Alex asked. "I've got some beer. Or do you have to get up early in the morning?"

"I'm off tomorrow," I replied. *This night might not be a waste after all,* I thought happily.

It was going on a quarter to four when we finally went inside. He unzipped his jacket and pulled it off.

It was then that I realized that I only had my *under armour* top, pants, and underwear on. Although they were great for keeping me warm, I didn't think they'd be quite so great for just sitting and chilling over our beers.

Alex just chuckled and vanished into his bedroom. A few moments later, he came back out—having changed from his jeans into sweatpants—and brought out a clean tee-shirt and shorts, and then waved me into the bathroom so I could change into something warm and dry. Once I got back to the living room, there was a cold beer sitting on the coffee table for me. By now I was overheating and needed it. It seemed like he did to because we both downed it like it was water.

Alex quickly got two more out of the fridge.

So here I was, sitting and drinking beer with this extremely hot guy and I'm a light drinker so after I'd downed my third beer, I was getting a lot less shy. I decided to test the waters. We'd been talking sports for a while now—he had played college football. "So, what kind of porn do you like?"

"I've one in the DVD player right now," Alex replied. "Do you want to watch it while we talk?"

"Sure." I grinned at him.

"It's a mixture of scenes I like."

The television warmed up and the video began to play. It was girl-on-girl to start with, but soon changed to girl-on-guy.

By now we were both on our fifth beer each, and luckily for me he was wearing jogging pants and I could see he was becoming very horny from the porn. Of course, I was rocking a hard-on of my own the whole time because I could tell that he was in at least decent shape through those loose clothes.

During this whole time, neither of us made an attempt to rub our cocks. So I stood up and announced that I was headed to the washroom.

As I was coming down the hallway, I could see his hand rubbing his crotch and thought that he couldn't take it anymore and was trying to rub one out before I got back. I didn't want him to stop; I was hoping to see if I could watch him shoot his load. It was hard to tell just how big he was from this angle, but I could see that his had a nice solid smooth head and oozing out of it was a nice amount of pre-cum. I wanted to see how long and thick he was so I moved down a bit further and caught a glimpse of the TV.

There on Alex's television screen was this muscle jock with a ten inch cock fucking another muscle jock with a ten inch cock.

I couldn't believe my eyes. I thought I was hard before, but this made my cock grow even harder.

Now, I'd been with guys before, but they were ones I'd picked up at parties, or in bars or online. I was not used to just coming onto them in their own living room. George not withstanding. I didn't want to just sit there all night either so I decided to make my presence known.

I backed up a bit further into the hallway. "Do you want another beer?" I called out.

"Sure," Alex replied. I could hear him struggling to get his cock stuffed back into his pants.

When I walked back into the living room, he had turned off the porn and was just sitting there.

I gave him the beer, pretending not to notice anything. In reality, I was studying him as much as I dared. I could tell that his cock was still sticking out of his pants and he had it covered by his shirt. I knew that he had at least seven inches hidden away, and a decent thickness from the outline.

I sat down beside him and we cracked open the beers and kept drinking and talking. I found out that he hasn't had sex since he'd moved in.

"Yeah, it's been over a month since I got a piece." Alex took a long drink. "I'm just not having much luck meeting anyone. I'm too shy I think."

"Why would you be shy?"

"I just am. That's why the porn is always in the DVD player."

I chuckled. "I haven't managed to score in quite a while either," I told him. "Probably been closer to four months for me."

'Four months,' he mouthed, then his jaw dropped open. "Christ, how can you go that long without sex?" He shook his head. "I mean, really. How can you do it? Or not do it? Shit, I'd break down and pay for someone if I had gone that long."

"Well, it does hurt after a while, but I just jerk off a lot." I was watching closely and I could see his cock twitched. "You know what's it like when you get horny."

"Yeah." Alex licked his lips.

"So, why is the porn off?"

"DVD ended."

"Oh." It's over." I grabbed the remote and pressed *play*. "So, let's watch it over again." I was really hoping that the gay scene was still on, and it was.

Alex turned red in the face right away but he didn't make a move to turn it off or anything—it was like he was waiting to see what I would do.

I certainly didn't disappoint him.

> I slide my hands down into my pants and started rubbing my
> cock. By this point, I was somewhere around six beers in and
> I'd lost all inhibition. Or so I could claim later on.

Alex looked over and his faced turned back to normal color and he smiled.

He didn't hesitate at all. He stood up and took his pants completely off and his cock was just beautiful—to this day it is the prettiest cock I've ever seen in person or porn. Its eight-plus inches was the perfect thickness, and the cock head was so smooth without any scars anywhere. It cured upwards, as I found out later, meant that he hit the spot every time when he fucked me on my back. He had nice medium hanging balls which were perfect for doggy-style, so I could hear those balls slap against me. And as if it couldn't get any better, he shaved his whole cock area. I didn't waste anytime getting more comfortable, off came all my clothes and when I sat back down I made sure that I sat a little closer.

He took his shirt off and put his right hand on my left thigh and slowly moved his hand up and down. Seeing as how I started off by my taking my clothes off I figured that I had to keep one step ahead of him, so I slid my left hand just about his cock and massaged the edges slightly touch his ball sack, which jumped each time.

It wasn't about ten seconds later that we were stroking each other to the rhythm of the men fucking on the DVD, with each thrust of his hands I had to hold back harder then I ever had so not to cum. Not wanting this to be over I decided to make a move to suck his beautiful pre-cum covered cock.

I took my hand off his cock and turned towards him. I moved his leg up over me and then leaned him on his back and grabbed his cock with my right hand and grasped his balls with my left.

Alex was wearing a big, encouraging smile.

I leaned in and took a big long smell; I wanted to savor ever moment of my first experience with his beautiful cock. He smelled exactly like I would after physical labor for two hours. But for some reason it made me hornier then ever—coming from him it was sweetness. I first started to lick his balls while I stroked his cock long and slow, not wanting him to cum to fast.

I sucked on them for at least five minutes, maybe longer, and he was moaning softly which told me he was liking every moment of it. Once I had enough of them I started to move my tongue up his thick shaft making sure to kiss every inch of his manhood. His cock was almost to hot to touch, and once I got to the head I instantly tasted a nice thick, sweet pre-cum. I always heard other guys complain that cum was salty but his tasted sweet, and I was glad it did. I was so nervous that I wouldn't like the taste of cum that I hesitated on going right to sucking, but once I tasted his, down it when.

I almost got it all the way down, and I loved it. The warmth in my mouth, the way the soft head of the cock touched the back of my throat, it all felt so good!

I made sure to play with his balls the whole time because I know how much I liked someone doing that to me and it always made me cum so much harder. I was glad to hear, from that moaning, that Alex liked it as well.

"Oh yeah, Mason," he groaned. "Just keep doing that." He was thrusting his hips upward at a faster and faster pace, and I knew he was going to cum soon, I didn't care anymore, I got the feeling that I could trust him, seeing as I now had my cock in his mouth—it was only later that I found out I was right—I pulled up and asked if he liked to top?

"Oh, fuck, do I ever!" He gave me a grin. "Do you want me to cum inside you?"

"Yeah."

This guy was fucking amazing. He knew exactly what I wanted. "Be gentle, it's been a while."

"But you have done this before?"

"Yeah, I've been fucked before. Played with my ass and it can take a dildo, just not one as big as you."

"I'll take my time. You won't feel any pain."

Seeing as we didn't prepare for this, he thought it would be good to just push his cock against my ass and push lightly until it slid all the way in.

I can still remember exactly how felt, as I lay on my back on the carpet, with him on atop of me, facing me, and how much I loved it.

Alex was about halfway into me. "I'm not gonna be able to hang on for long," he gasped.

"That's okay. I'm getting close too." I really was. "If you stroke my cock a few times, I'll cum too! Go right ahead and feed me that cock."

Alex's smile grew even bigger and so did his cock.

I'd swear it grew half an inch. He fucked me long and slow, almost taking his cock all the way out before sliding it back down to almost the base.

He just started pumping me faster and I knew he was gonna cum; I looked up at him and told him to jerk my cock when he's ready to cum. About three pumps later he wraps his hand around my cock and starts to stroke it fast, as soon as he did this, I squeezed my ass to tight that he nearly fell on top of me as he grunted and groaned for a good minute, thrust himself at me harder each time as he shot load after load of hot sweet cum up my ass.

Then he really did collapse, laying there on top of me, his hot body pressed against mine, his big cock still in my tight ass. I could tell he was still hard and he slowly fucked me for another few minutes before he remembered that he had let go of my cock and that I still hadn't cum. Without pulling out, he reached down took hold of my own erection with his hand. He started jerking my cock while suck my head so fucking hard.

It only took about thirty seconds for me to shudder. "I'm—" I gasped before white goo splashed into his palm and splattered across my stomach. "God," I moaned, "I haven't cum like that in ages."

Alex was looking down at me, still smiling. "Glad that you enjoyed it," he said. He let go of me and lifted his hand to his lips. "Do you mind if I cum again?" he asked. "Before we stop for the night, I mean?"

"Not at all." God, I didn't ever want him to stop what he was doing.

So Alex just kept on fucking me. This time, of course, it took him a little bit longer. I shifted positions, going from laying on my back to my knees and hands, and my god, it felt so good to have a strong man behind me, hands on my waist feeding me his cock..

It took Alex about ten minutes for him to feed me more of his cum, but I didn't mind. I could have let him do that all night.

Once he came he pushed me down flat on the floor and just laid on top of me for a few minutes, it felt so good to feel him go soft inside me, and I couldn't believe how fucking good it felt when he popped it out.

We got cleaned up and had a few more beers, by this time it was about eight in the morning, with the sun coming through the clouds. We were both pretty done with and we decided to call it a night.

I got all my stuff together, and then paused with my hand on the door handle. "You should come over after you wake up."

"Yeah?"

"Well, I owe you for the beers. We can watch some porn too."

Alex gave me a sly smile. "Is around four a good time?"

"Oh yeah...the door will be unlocked."

On the way out, he grabbed my ass and reached around and grabbed my cock through my pants. "This was the best fuck I've ever had. I'm looking forward to having a third round at four."

I was hard again in my own pants, but I really was too tired to do anything about it. "I'll see you in eight hours."

Chapter Six

I was just returning to the store from a delivery. Since all transactions were

prepaid before delivery, all that the company routine required me to do was get a signature from the customer confirming delivery and check in with the accounting office upon returning. The reason for this was that occasionally a customer wasn't home when I made a delivery, and when something had to come back it played hell with the books.

"Hi, Joan," I said, striding into the accounting office.

Joan, the accountant, never let me hear the end of it when I had to bring something back. We were both in our late twenties and still caught fast in the silliness of youth, which is probably why we got along so well.

Now she turned to me and smiled sweetly, launching her attack. "Bring anything back this time?"

"Hey, two times out of seventy-seven deliveries so far makes about a two point six percent rate of non-deliverable goods."

She gave me a comically sceptical look. "That doesn't matter when it happens twice in a row. Nice work with the math, by the way. Where'd you hide your calculator?"

I pulled it out of my inside jacket pocket and held it up, smiling at her. "Can't pull anything over you, can I?"

She shook her head, laughing. "No, and you still haven't answered my question."

"No, nothing this time." I replaced my calculator and handed her the sheaf of office copies for the receipts, keeping the other set of copies for the delivery records.

"So how'd it go this time?" she asked, checking through the office copies and quickly updating the records on her computer.

I made notes in my own record book from my own set of copies, marking off the invoice numbers. "Not too bad. This time of day the traffic is pretty close to nonexistent. That's how I like it, too."

"Me, too. Even on my twenty-minute drive every morning and every evening I encounter a million idiots on the road. I've seen enough accidents to last me a lifetime."

I finished with the copies, clipping them to the back of my clipboard until I could put them away in the shipping office files. "I've seen a few, too. Some nasty ones."

Just then, I heard the voice of my employer, Lochlyn, page me to his office over the intercom.

"That's me," I told Joan.

"That's you," she agreed, mocking my tone. "You had better hurry. Lochlyn doesn't like to be kept waiting."

"Yes, dear," I said sarcastically, grinning and starting to leave.

An eraser flew at my head, and I ducked as it bounced off of a wall and landed in the garbage can. I waved to an evilly-grinning Joan and headed down the hallway, double-checking my record book.

As I rounded a corner I nearly ran into a man going in the opposite direction. "Sorry," I said, looking up from my book.

"Excuse me," he said as he went past. Out of the corner of my eye I happened to note that he disappeared into the washroom. As I continued walking to Lochlyn's office, I could still see the man's face in my mind's eye. Tall, about my height, dark hair, light blue eyes, sharp features, very light stubble on his face. Probably about twenty-five or so, just at a rough guess. The word "cute" didn't come to mind; "cute" was what I thought of when I thought of baby rabbits and puppies and kittens. Not drop-dead gorgeous, either, just quite
pleasant-looking.

I knocked on Lochlyn's open door, noting him up to his ears in paperwork. He didn't look up at me. "Come on in, Mason."

I sat down in the extra chair.

"Everything go all right?" he asked, finally looking up.

I nodded. "I just got back. I got everything delivered all right."

"Good, good." He nodded his head. "We've got a new guy working here. He starts today as a sort of maintenance man for the back. His name is Daryn, and I've told him you can help him settle in to the routine here. Just show him around, help him if he needs supplies—you know, the basics."

"Not a problem," I said. "Things usually aren't so busy that I can't take a few minutes out here and there."

Just then the man I had almost run into walked into Lochlyn's office.

I hid my sudden surprise, and confirmed for myself that he was really quite good-looking.

Lochlyn gave the new guy a smile. "Ah, Daryn. This is Mason, our primary delivery man. He'll help you settle in. Mason, this is Daryn."

Daryn turned to me and said, "Hi."

We shook hands.

Lochlyn looked at me. "Well, you know what to do. I'll check back with you in a little while to see how things are going." He chuckled. "It's all this paperwork keeping me bogged down right now."

Daryn was grinning. "It's all never-ending."

"I thought we were supposed to be a paperless society, but you'd never know it fro my desk most days."

I smiled and nodded, then left. I looked behind me and saw Daryn catching up to me. I asked him, "Well, what do you think?"

He looked thoughtfully at me. "About the job, you mean?"

"Yeah."

He pondered a moment. "It's a living," he said, chuckling to himself.

I gave him a matching grin. "Well, you've got the right attitude. Now I know you've got a chance of surviving the job. Now you have to survive your coworkers, most of whom I'm sure are criminally insane."

"Yourself included?"

I thought a moment. "Can you take the Fifth only in the United States?"

He paused. "I think so."

"Then I just have no comment."

Daryn laughed again. "Are they really that bad?"

"Well, they just take some getting used to. Their sense of humour is no exception to this."

I poked my head into Joan's office on the way past. "Hi there," I said.

"You again?" she said, jokingly. "I thought I just got rid of you."

"No such luck, my dear." I laughed. "I'm too tenacious." I waited until she rolled her eyes. "Joan, this is Daryn, our new maintenance guy. Daryn, this is Joan. She's our accountant, so if you're sent on an errand you need money for, she's the one to see."

"*'Tenacious'*?" Joan asked, smiling. "Big word. Looked it up in the dictionary to see what it meant so I'd think you're smart, huh?"

I smiled back. "No, I looked it up to try to confuse you, but I don't have to use words half that long to confuse you."

She laughed as we left. "Got that right. At least today, anyways. See you around."

I looked at Daryn, who was watching our exchange with a bemused expression on his face. "We bug each other all the time. Keeps us sane."

He nodded, smiling and shaking his head as though wondering what he'd gotten himself into.

We finally reached the shipping office. Brett, the shipping manager, looked at me from behind his desk. "So I see that Lochlyn has you playing teacher, huh?"

I lowered my voice, in an aside to Daryn. "See what I mean?" I raised my voice as I called back to Brett, "Better than playing seat warmer." That evoked laughs and chuckles from around the shipping room.

Andrew, one of the other dock workers, called to me, "Hey Mason, smack him one if he doesn't behave." He pointed his thumb back at Brett.

I shook my head. "God, if he liked it then I'd never get rid of him." That brought more laughs.

Brett picked up a pencil and hurled it playfully across the room at me.

I put my hand on the back of Daryn's neck and said, "Duck!" We dropped to the floor as the pencil whizzed overhead and hit the door, its graphite tip shattering on the painted metal surface before it fell piecemeal to the floor. I picked it up and stood up, calling to Brett, "I think Mattel makes unbreakable toys you could benefit from." More laughs followed me and Daryn to the records room.

Unbreakable toys weren't really on my mind as I started filing the shipping copies, explaining to Daryn what I was doing. Remembering the feel of his firm shoulder muscles under my hand had raised thoughts of what the rest of his body must be like. If his shoulders were any indication as to what the rest of his body was like, then I had just touched the tip of the iceberg, so to speak.

"So, will I be expected to take care of the records as well?" he asked.

"Not so much. Occasionally, but most of the time I'll be able to take care of this. You'll be more in charge of making sure all the stock is in good shape, reporting any damaged stock either to Brett or to Lochlyn, running the occasional errand—pretty generic stuff, really. You shouldn't have too much problem."

"Mason!" came Brett's voice. "Delivery!"

"Another one?" I mused aloud. "Hmm...that's strange. I thought I had done all the day's jobs." I shrugged. "It was probably being processed while I was out."

I went and checked with Brett. It was rare that this happened, having one delivery almost immediately after the other. I didn't mind, though. It just meant that my own paperwork would have to be delayed until a bit later.

I waited while Brett arranged to have the delivery loaded. I turned to Daryn and

said, "Go back and check with Mitch. He's the short red-haired guy. He'll let you know what to do with this delivery."

I waited until Brett gave me the papers, then headed into the back to get ready to go.

I walked into the stock room to find the bay door open to the warm summer air. The delivery truck was still backed into the bay, its cargo bay open and waiting to be loaded. My attention, however, was focused on something else. Mitch and Daryn were lifting a couch into the back of the truck.

I couldn't take my eyes off of Daryn. Under the fabric of his jeans, which were slim but not really tight, his leg muscles bulged and flexed powerfully. I could see a similar sight under his shirt, where his muscles, when they flexed, stretched the fabric in many places to the contours of his body. It was a beautiful sight to behold.

When they were finished, I walked over to Daryn. "If you need something else to do, just ask Mitch or Brett or Andrew or Lochlyn. Lochlyn should be coming back here sometime soon to see how you're getting used to things, anyways. All right?"

"Okay." He seemed a bit on edge. I could relate; the first day on a job was usually confusing until the routine sunk in.

I put on my sunglasses to see through the glare outside, fired up the truck, and left on my delivery, with thoughts of Daryn's robust body on my mind.

The delivery went without incident. I managed to ignore a raging hard-on spawned by my thoughts of what Daryn must look like without any clothes on. By the time I was back at work, I had managed to obviate my "tension" back to non-existence.

I strode into Joan's office and said, "Yes, it got delivered fine."

She just smiled at me. "What made you think I was going to ask you anything regarding your delivery?"

"Just a feeling I had," I said, smiling and feigning suspicion. "I'm training myself as a psychic, if you must know."

The rest of the day passed fairly uneventfully. I spent what remaining time there was in the records room sorting copies and keeping track of them in a computer database. I had to stay perhaps five minutes past five in order to finish up, and something caught the corner of my eye. I looked up and noticed Daryn standing there.

"Hi, Mason," he said. "Hope I'm not disturbing you."

"I'm just finishing up anyways. So how did today go?"

"Not too bad. It'll take me a bit to get into the routine, though."

I smiled. "Brett being a shit again?"

He laughed a little. "I wouldn't say that."

I shook my head. "You don't know him well enough yet."

Daryn laughed again. "Can I ask you a favour?"

"Sure."

"I had to get a ride here today. Can I catch a ride home with you? I don't live far from here."

I looked around me. "If you can stand to wait about five more minutes, then I have no problem."

"Thanks a lot. My car had to go in for some work today." He chuckled.

"You know how people get if they can't see your brake lights working."

"Good thing you had them worked on today. The police are out in full force today for some reason. Must be a full moon or something tonight."

"Must be."

It didn't even take five minutes before I was finished. I saved the records, logged out of the system, and we left.

Daryn directed me as we drove over to his house. On the way I found out that he was twenty-five—my guess had been right on—and not presently attached to anyone in any way—although he had dated occasionally throughout and after high school—and that we shared some interests in music, reading, hobbies, and the need for quiet time alone every now and then. He tended to be quiet and introverted as I was at times. I wondered for a moment if it weren't for the same reason. Thankful for sunglasses, I was able to hide my eye movements as I rested my gaze upon his legs and his crotch several times.

Still, all too soon I was pulling up in front of his apartment building where he lived. "So, do you need a ride to work tomorrow?"

He thought a moment. "No, I should be okay tomorrow, thanks."

"Okay, call me if you do though." I fumbled a pen from the dash and scrawled my number on the back of a fast food receipt.

Then I head home.

Once home, I heated up some leftovers for dinner, watched some TV, then read a bit
before crashing for the day.

The next day at work, Brett called me over to his desk. I had another few things to deliver, and he was just obtaining the address for me.

"Here it is," he said, pulling up the screen on his terminal.

I looked at it and tried to picture a map of the city in my mind. Finally it clicked. I said, "Rural address. That's way outside the city, isn't it?"

He nodded. "Yeah, about twenty kilometres southeast. Need a map?"

"No, it's not too far from where I live. I know the area."

"All right." His grin turned impish. "Then move your butt, already."

I swatted him on the back of the head. "Someone forgot to tell you that a long time ago, I think."

I looked at my watch. It read 11:47. "I haven't had lunch yet," I commented. "I'm going to stop and have something on the way back, all right?"

"Fair enough," Brett replied. "I'm going to be taking off for a bit in a minute or two here, too."

Daryn was standing near the door. "If you're going for lunch, can I go with you?" he asked. "I didn't bring anything."

"That all right, Brett?" I asked. "Your call."

"You've got an hour, right?" Brett asked Daryn.

"Yep." Daryn nodded.

"All right, you know when you've got to be back here, then."

A few minutes later, we were on our way. The day was warm and clear, and I had to don my sunglasses again to keep the glare down.

Daryn cleared his throat. "On the way back, can we stop and pick up my car?"

"Sure. Just let me know where it is after we're finished this delivery."

We were quickly outside of city limits and on the rural highways. I was able to sneak a few more peeks at Daryn's body on the way while we talked. It was one of those bodies that you just couldn't look at enough.

He was nicely built, well proportioned, and was quite good-looking on top of it all. My crotch started to stir again.

A few kilometres later, we came over a hill and saw a construction zone ahead. The traffic line-up wasn't overly long, but it was the principle of having to wait. I let out my breath slowly to indicate mild annoyance. I tried to divert myself by checking out each of the construction workers to see if there was anyone I knew among them. I'd met up with one or two members of the hardhat brigade and they'd been great in bed.

Within about ten minutes we were under way again, but by that time I was noticeably more annoyed at having been delayed.

"Tense?" Daryn asked me.

"No, I'm fine," I denied, letting out my breath again. I was quickly getting it out of my mind.

"I don't mean tense, I mean...tense." With that, his hand came to rest on my crotch. Simultaneously, he took one of my hands from the steering wheel and placed it onto his denim-covered crotch, where my suspicions of ample padding were amply confirmed.

I was taken completely aback. I had forgotten about my hard-on down there. I looked over at him for an explanation.

He pulled my sunglasses off, making me squint against the sudden glare. "You really overestimate how much these hide your eye movements." His face split in a wide, sexy grin as he started to squeeze and massage my crotch, turning up the heat.

I turned my attention back to the road. I was in familiar territory; this wasn't too far from where I lived. I knew many of the back roads quite well. I decided to take one that wasn't used too much, but would still be easy for a large truck to get out of without getting stuck in a rut or in the grass.

Once we were off the highway a fair distance, I parked the truck and shut off the engine. I knew there would be no traffic along here; it was a dead-end road that just led to a field by a marshy lake anyways. I waited to see what Daryn would do.

I didn't have to wait long.

He slid over right next to me, put his other hand on the back of my neck, and pressed his lips into mine. I closed my eyes under the force of the feeling that swept over me. Since I couldn't use my eyes to explore his body, I had to rely on my other senses, such as touch. I slid one hand down his strong torso and managed to pop his jeans open far enough to slide my hand in. Under his briefs lay a well-padded treasure, slowly beginning to awaken and

just waiting to be teased.

His fingers found their way through my button-fly as well and began slipping the buttons open, one by one. His hand slipped inside and started massaging my cock and balls through my underwear. It only sent another rush of hormones flooding through my body.

I pulled back from our kiss and began unbuttoning his shirt. I clumsily managed to get one button undone with my free hand before giving up and using my mouth to undo them. I may not have been much more dexterous with my tongue and lips, but I certainly enjoyed it more. Daryn's soft moans indicated he did as well. After undoing each button, I began softly kissing and licking my way down to the next one. He kept moving back so I could have more room to stretch out on the seat and reach lower and lower each time.

When I finally got the last button undone, I went back to the area around the sparse patch of dark hairs between his firm, well-rounded pecs. I planted light kisses here and there and over his pecs, not ignoring his nipples, now firm and pointed. I teased each one with my tongue, listening to his deep, steady breathing become quick gasps with each caress.

I slowly followed where the hairs led down to a thin, downy trail that disappeared under his briefs. I tugged at them with my teeth, noting the hard outline pointing up at an angle underneath. I began pulling more insistently, wanting to reach what lay hidden under the fabric.

"Hang on a sec," he said. I sat up while he first took off one shoe so he could slip one leg out of his jeans. He pulled his shirt off and laid it on the windowsill as a pillow. He rested his head back against it, his free leg up on the seat. I leaned over him again, gave

him a deep, full-mouthed kiss, then planted kisses again down his chest towards his pulsing crotch. I used my lips to tug lightly at the trail of hair that disappeared into his underwear, listening to his breathing go from steady to erratic and back to steady again.

I pulled slowly yet insistently at his underwear, ever so slowly sliding them down his hips. His cock kept throbbing and pushing at his briefs, as though it had a mind of its own and wanted out. I was more than happy to oblige. I seized it in my lips through the fabric and massaged it for a few moments before pulling his briefs down far enough to expose his treasure.

He brought his free leg up so I could slip it completely out of his underwear. Waiting for my attention when he brought his leg back down was about eight inches of rock-solid manhood, so hard it barely even moved with each pulse of his heart. The scent of his musk assaulted my senses, sending my hormones sky-high. I began tracing the contours of his shaft with my tongue, leaving a thin, shiny trail of saliva along it. With every touch of my tongue he let out a long, low moan, somewhere between a sigh and a growl.

I put my lips against one of his balls and created a light suction in my mouth strong enough to lift it up into my mouth. I traced my tongue over it, listening to his moans become louder. I released him from my mouth and did the same to the other one, alternating the two back and forth. I placed the tip of my tongue on the fold of skin between his ass and his balls, right close to his asshole, and traced a thin, wavering line up and across the fold and up over his balls. I continued up the length of his pulsating cock until I reached the swollen, sensitive head. Even the light touch of my breath was enough to make his breathing sound laboured from the depths of his hormone-filled body.

I began massaging along the length of his cock with my lips, starting at the head. I wanted to tease him for as long as possible. He tasted musky, almost sweet. I took one final run up the length of his shaft with my tongue before enfolding the head of his cock with my

lips and drawing about half of his swollen cock into my mouth. His moan was almost a helpless whimper.

I drew back so I only had the head in my mouth, then began curling my tongue around it again. I ran the tip of my tongue around the crown, over his cock-hole, over the frenum, then back around again. I could virtually sense what his prick looked like even more clearly than if I'd used my eyes. I wanted to see it in more detail; I wanted to spend hours holding him at the edge of release, studying his every physical detail with the sense of touch. I knew he wouldn't be able to hold out that long; even since I'd started working him over his arousal level had jumped about a hundredfold. He had a few minutes left, at most.

I wanted to make the most of those few minutes, so I kept the pace slow, gentle, tender. I released him from my hold, licked my lips, then gently slid his rod into my throat as far as I could. I had him virtually all the way down, with his pubes brushing against the tip of my nose. I kept most of him in my mouth while I began to suck him off. I used my fingernails to rake firmly yet gently along his powerful, goosebump-covered thighs as his body alternately tensed and relaxed in the depths of ecstasy. He was pushing his hips upwards slightly each time I went down on him, and his breathing was no longer following a

regular pace. I snuck a peek at him, noting he had lolled his head back over the seat and had closed his eyes, his tongue slowly tracing around his lips.

I decided to help him release his tension, so I first slowly increased the pressure I was exerting with my lips, turning up the friction. Then

I took my middle finger and began tracing around the rim of his ass, gently tickling the sensitive skin there. I slowly began working my finger into his asshole, hearing his moans intensify. Before long I had my finger entirely inside him, pressing on his swollen prostate. It drove him wild. He was approaching the point of no return, and very quickly, too. His breathing had gone beyond erratic and now sounded like it was a life-draining effort to keep his lungs filled with fresh air. He started making whimpering noises, his body now continually shuddering with pure sexual tension on the verge of bursting loose.

Daryn let out a low, forceful moan. I barely heard him breathe, "Oh, fuck," before he tensed up completely and cried out. His cock swelled suddenly in my mouth and contracted again. One small spurt was followed by a thick stream of hot, sweet liquid that seemed to fill my mouth with the first gush. I quickly swallowed his spunk which, judging from the volume, had obviously been building up in his balls for quite some time, and then caught the rest of it as it literally flowed from his body.

I kept my lips around him until his prick stopped its spasms. I raised myself up to him, wrapped my arms around his robust torso, and pressed my mouth into his, where I shared with him the gift he'd given me. Our tongues seemed insistent on painting the insides of our mouths with his cum, our bodies melding into one with the heat we'd generated between us.

He was far from finished, though. His body easily overpowered mine—not that I was trying to resist him, mind you—and he gently pushed me down on the bench-seat so we were lying down, him on top of me. His sexy eyes and smile fixed on me, he murmured seductively, "Now it's your turn."

He slid his hands under my shirt and slipped it up and off of my body, pulling it easily over my arms. He turned his attention to my neck, one of my sensitive spots. His lips and tongue traced intricate lines while he slipped one hand down my bare chest to the top of my pants, which he'd already undone. His hand slid under my briefs, seized my still-hard shaft, and started stroking it. He moved down to it and let his hot breath flow over it, caressing it more gently than the most delicate flesh-to-flesh contact could ever hope to. He

substituted a stroking hand with a stroking tongue, making long, slow licks over my balls and cock. He pulled at my pants and briefs, a signal at which I lifted my hips up far enough for him to pull my pants and underwear down around my knees. He gave my cock a few

tentative strokes with his hand before replacing it with his mouth. I could tell from his actions that he wasn't among the more experienced cocksuckers, but his mouth felt so hot and velvety soft it was like having the world's best cocksucker working on my prick. At this rate I wouldn't last very long at all.

He was mimicking some of my actions, swirling his tongue around my cockhead. I thought nothing of it; that was how I had learned to suck cock properly. I hadn't expected him to open his mouth and let a mouthful of saliva drench my cock, though.

He moved up to me and kissed me again.

I chuckled. "Tired out?"

He shook his head slightly. "Fuck me," he whispered seductively.

I suddenly understood why he'd drenched my cock with saliva. "You sure?" I asked him.

He nodded, his eyes closed in desire. "If just your finger felt like it did, then I want to see what *you* will feel like."

I smiled at him and nodded slightly. He allowed me to get to a sitting position on the seat before turning around and getting on all fours, facing away from me.

I cupped my hand under my balls to catch some of his saliva. I rubbed it over my prick, then spat into my hand and applied it to his ass, working his ass muscles open slightly with two fingertips. I pressed my cockhead into his waiting ass and held it there.

"Let me know if it becomes uncomfortable," I told him.

Daryn's head turned partly back towards me, he nodded.

I pressed slightly harder, feeling his hole resist slightly. He moaned, so I waited a moment before continuing. I pushed a bit more and felt him start to open up. By pushing and waiting, pushing and waiting, I slowly worked my cock into him so that just my cockhead was inside his ass.

Just then he reached back, grabbed my hips, and pushed back into me quickly and forcefully. He let out a loud, guttural cry, not a cry of pain but a cry of pleasure. Even so, it took me a moment to be sure.

"You all right?" I asked him.

He nodded. "Better than I ever imagined..." he trailed off.

With my prick buried inside his hot asshole, I ran my hands up his sides and around his chest and over his shoulders. I pulled his torso up to a backward-reclining position. His asshole tightened up around my cock once he was in the upright position, and there was still room for me to fuck him slowly in this position. I ran my hands over his chest and nipples, finding all his erogenous zones one at a time. His cock was coming back to life, too, which didn't entirely surprise me.

I began fucking him slowly, gently, allowing him time to relax since what he'd said had all but given me a written confession that he'd never been fucked before. I grabbed his cock and began stroking it, slowly starting to jerk him off. He slid his hands back around to my butt cheeks, where he started massaging them gently.

I was so horny by this point that I started jerking him off faster and harder, pushing gently into him, until he started to moan again. He cried out and arched his back, his head lolling back over my shoulder. In a wave of hormones, I pushed my prick hard into him. I could feel his dick swell slightly in my hand and his cum began pumping out again. It spurted up his stomach and painted his abs in white spatters from the thin patch of black chest hairs down into his pubic hairs, where a slow stream of cum was flowing out his prick-slit, over my hand, and pooling into his pubic hair. His hands came around to his front and seized mine, and our hands began rubbing his cum all over his stomach and chest.

We began to clean up, using only our briefs so that any unsightly and embarrassing cum-stains wouldn't be visible later. We only wiped off our hands, just so we wouldn't get

it all over the place. Then he whispered in my ear, "Now fuck me hard. Not rough, but hard."

I understood what he meant. I waited for him to lean forward and brace himself on the seat again. I put my hands on his slim waist and began sliding my cock in and out of his ass. There was nothing rough about the way it went. I pushed forcefully but steadily into him and slid back out, then paused slightly before continuing. His moans signalled approval. I was using my whole body from the knees up for momentum, propelling myself deep inside his body without bouncing roughly off of his ass cheeks. I slowly started to increase the pace, starting to keep most of my body immobile while using only my hips to

drive my shaft into him. His hot, hungry ass was just like his mouth: warm, velvety soft, and getting me even hotter. I was getting close really quickly.

Just then I could feel my balls tensing up and getting ready to explode. I said, "I'm gonna blow..." and gasped the last word out. Just as my cock contracted in climax and I could feel my cum boiling out of my balls, it felt like tons of the stuff came rushing out my

cock, expanding it beyond its normal capacity. Out of reflex I pushed into him so deeply I thought I would ram my balls inside his ass, too.

I must have kept myself there for what seemed like twenty minutes, my shaft still shuddering inside him, cum still oozing out of my cock-slit, my eyes closed tightly in almost unbearable pleasure.

I slowly pulled out of him, my prick incredibly sensitive. As my prick popped out of his ass he turned over and wrapped his arms around me, kissing me deeply and pulling me down to the seat on top of him.

"I don't need lunch now. I've had my protein infusion."

I laughed. "Yeah, but you also lost a lot in the process. And I mean a *lot*."

"I know, I was bit pent up." He giggled, then kissed me again.

"Down boy, I said with more than a bit of reluctance. "We gotta get this furniture delivered."

"All right, Mason, but I've got plans to see you after you work." Daryn gave me a smile and gentle squeezed my crotch. "Once we get together in some place more comfortable than the cab of a delivery truck."

"You've got yourself a date," I told him.

Chapter Seven

Maria was about the eighth person to see the rental house that day. There had been a pretty steady stream of folks since the open house started. Most couples overlapped, which was good—it created a sense of competition. Now, though, she was the only one and the open house was, officially, over.

"The only problem," she said, "is that we had an eviction a year ago when my husband was out of work. Other than that, our record's clean."

"I'm sorry," I told her. "My criteria has worked out pretty well in the past and I think I'll stick with it. I'm sure there's a landlord out there somewhere who'll rent to you."

"But I really want this house. It's just the right size and it's close to the kids' school and babysitter. Is there any way you could overlook that eviction?"

"Sorry," I replied.

She glanced around and then looked back at me. "I'll do *anything* to change your mind," she continued, emphasizing the word 'anything'. "Really, anything," she said as she stood and spread her legs a bit and hiked her skirt a few inches.

She was attractive, that's for sure—short Latina with long, straight black hair, nice tits and ass, but pussy just wasn't my game. I had to laugh—I got hit on by the ladies often enough. They think just because a guy is masculine—some have said I look *'rugged'*, whatever that means—that he's straight. And I love to see the look on their faces when I set them—no pun intended—straight.

"Lady, you're barking up the wrong tree. You've got nothing down there that interests me." Then, as a joke I added, "Now if your husband's as hot as you and willing to make a similar offer, maybe we could arrange something."

She muttered something in Spanish I didn't understand. The only part I heard was an emphasis on the words "mi casa."

Sadly she was the last person to stop by, and the realtor just gave a shrug when she stopped by to pick up her 'open house' signs.

I stayed around for about an hour to work on a closet door in the master bedroom that kept coming off its track.

The doorbell rang.

"Who can that be?" I walked down the hallway, frowning to myself. The bell rang again. I pull the door open and stared.

The man on the doorstep was well-built, with dark hair and a heavy tan.

"Hi," he said, in a deep voice flavoured with a heavy Spanish accent. "My name is Juan. My Maria sent me here to do some work for you. She said she will have this house and I will do whatever you need." In his right hand was a toolbox and in his left hand an extension cord and a drill. He lifted his hands to show me he was ready to do whatever I needed him to do to get this house.

I couldn't help but stand there and stare. He was just the kind of guy that made me drool. He was about five six, solid build—not thin, not fat—with black hair, goateed with a backwards *Maple Leafs* baseball cap, tee-shirt, and jeans ripped at the knee. If I believed in a supreme gay being I would have thanked him for answering my prayers.

I was pretty sure Maria had not clearly explained what she had offered for this house, and my facetious—at least I thought it was—counter offer.

I smiled—in part because I was imagining what sort of fun I could have with Juan—but also in part because I was imagining how mad he was going to be at Maria when she finally had to explain to him what she was asking him to do. And although I really wanted to play with Juan physically, I really didn't want to play with him emotionally.

I knew the chances of getting a straight man—and one who was a total stranger at that—to submit to my wildest desires were nil.

"Juan, I'm sorry, but I think Maria misunderstood a joke I made. There's really no work here for you."

"No, Maria said I must come here and help and we will get the house. She told me this." Juan was emphatic.

"Juan, I'm sorry, really I have no work for you."

We stood there looking at each other, each waiting for the other to concede. I'd have sent him on his way but he was just too fucking cute! "Call Maria," I said, "and tell her I said there's no work here for you."

He pulled out his cell phone and said something to Maria. His first sentence—I'm guessing the question about this "misunderstanding" was mostly calm but with a bit of agitation. But the next words out of his mouth were quite an explosion.

I didn't need to understand Spanish to know she explained more clearly what he was there for. This heated conversation went on for a while.

I turned away and quietly slipped away. I didn't want to be around much longer, imaging how angry he would be. I went back to work on my closet door.

The yelling stopped and I heard his phone click shut—louder than I thought a cell phone could click. I expected to hear the front door open and close. Instead I heard the bedroom door open a bit wider.

I looked up, startled, and turned my head enough to see Juan standing there looking—well, I guess *resigned* would be the best word.

We both looked at each other for what seemed like an eternity when Juan spoke. "Maria said I must do this or we will not get the house. Maria wants this house. What must I do?"

I felt sorry for the guy, but hey, his wife was okay with it and he appeared to be quite willing—grudgingly but willing enough to stick around—so who was I to turn him down?

That, being totally honest, I was between boyfriends and I wasn't about to give up an opportunity to have fun with the kind of guy that I jerked off to every night before I fell asleep—alone.

But I did decide to give him a break. "Look," I said, "I'll make it easy on you. I'll just give you a blow job and you can go and tell Maria the house is hers, okay?"

He looked somewhat relieved but still not entirely sure of what to do next.

"Come over here," I told him.

He took a few steps closer and looked down at his feet.

"Take your shirt off," I said. I love to watch men undress. And I don't mind being the one to tell them what to do and when to do it.

Juan took off his tee-shirt and tossed it aside. My cock crawled a bit when I saw the tattoo of the serpent on his chest.

I undid his belt and then unzipped his pants. I was getting harder and more uncomfortable in my own jeans. I knelt down and pulled his jeans down around his workers' boots. I nuzzled his cock through his underwear with my nose and face. I could feel him starting to get hard. I looked up. His eyes were closed. He probably didn't want to watch himself being taken by a man, I supposed.

I slowly pulled his underwear down around his ankles. His plump, uncut cock started to spring slowly upward. Again, I nuzzled his cock with my nose, lips and face. I wondered how he felt having a bushy beard brush his cock for the first time. I grabbed his shaft and licked the tip of his cock, parting the foreskin with my tongue and touching the head just at the piss slit. I ran my tongue under the foreskin and all around his cock head as his cock continued to grow, getting harder, the foreskin receding.

Juan started making audible, shallow breaths, probably trying not to say "screw this" and run away. His eyes were closed even harder as if he were concentrating on something – concentrating on not enjoying this thing being done to him.

Suddenly he started to fall. His eyes flew open and his arms flew out as I sprang to my feet and steadied him. He was breathing harder.

"Don't worry, just lay down and relax." I held his arms and helped him sit down.

Then he laid back on the carpet.

He watched me as I untied his shoes, took them off and tossed them aside. I pulled off his socks, jeans, and underwear from around his ankles.

Then I took off my shirt and threw it on the pile of his clothes while he continued to watch me. Standing near his waist, I took off my shoes, socks, and slid down my own jeans. My stiff hard-on was obvious beneath my army green briefs. I pulled the waistband out, over my horizontal cock, and stepped out of my underwear. Whereas his cock was shorter, plump and uncut, mine was longer, thin and cut.

His eyes narrowed, probably as he wondered what I planned to do with my own cock. I spread his legs apart and bent his knees toward his waist. He stopped breathing—I'm sure imagining I had changed the rules and was intending to take his ass.

When I took his nut sack into my mouth he exhaled quickly, either relieved that I wasn't mounting an assault on his rear or from the feeling of having his balls given a warm, wet massage. Or maybe it was a combination of the two. I started gentle but quickly progressed to tonguing them rough—the way I like to have mined licked. I ran my lips along the bottom side of his rock hard shaft, going back and forth as if I were playing a harmonica. It wasn't long till the music started. First were the soft moans coming from deep in his throat. As I went back and forth from his balls to the tip of his cock the moans changed, accordingly—deep guttural sounds when I was at his balls and softer, lighter moans when I twirled my tongue around his cockhead.

With my left hand I reached up and rubbed my thumb back and forth over his right nipple. This must have felt good because eventually Juan took his left hand and did the same to the unoccupied one. After a few minutes of this, I reached my right hand down to the jar of *Vaseline* I was using to lubricate the closet door. I lubed my middle finger and slowly started to explore the first half inch of Juan's back door.

Suddenly Juan was quiet as if he weren't sure whether he liked this or not. I ran my finger in a circular motion just barely inside his hole. To take his mind off his ass, I worked his nipple harder and increased the intensity with which I tongue-batted his balls. The return of his moans told me I was going in the right direction. Still unsure of how he felt about the as splay I decided it was better to be bold than timid, so I ran my lubed pudgy fuck finger all the way in and started massaging his gland.

I enjoyed a shot of pre-cum as he inhaled loudly. It wasn't long, though before his moans returned with definitely greater intensity as I continued the assault on his nipple, cock, balls, and ass. The temperature in the room seemed to climb with the intensity of our play. Sweat slowly started to trickle down either side of his nut sack, down his ass crack, and onto the wrist of the hand with which I fingered his feel-good hole.

Juan's moans started to turn into words—first quite soft, almost prayer like, then with greater intensity and louder like a chant. "Me *vengo*, me *vengo*, me *vengo*." He started bucking his ass off the newly laid carpet, actively fucking my face. "Me *vengo*, me *vengo*, me *vengo*!"

Even without knowing Spanish I knew what he was saying. I loved the feel of his rock hard rod straining to go further and further down my throat. I worked his prostate harder knowing how good it feels to be pleasured from inside and out at the same time.

Juan moaned louder. "Me *vengo*, me *vengo*, ME *VENGO*!"

I could feel the hot cum ricochet off my throat, some sliding back down his shaft making it even slicker as he continued to pump and squirt. As Juan's cum filled my throat I shot my load onto whatever was in the firing line of my cock. It was an odd sensation to cum without anything touching my rod, and seemed almost like an out of body experience.

Juan continued to pump even after the squirting stopped. His ass fell back to the floor and stayed there, his body too exhausted to continue. It seemed it was all he could do to catch his breath and try to make some sense out of the way his body participated willingly in this sensual, sexual feast despite the initial grave misgivings of his mind.

I ran my tongue one last time around Juan's cockhead beneath the foreskin. Then, as much as I didn't want to, I released the once-again flaccid cock from my mouth, returning it to its rightful owner. I felt almost sad thinking I would never enjoy the taste of his cum, the pleasure of watching him react to new sexual experiences. But, it was one of those things—just enjoy the moment.

As it turned out, it wasn't the last time we'd be together. Not by a long shot. In the six years since Maria told me the house would be hers, we've all sort of fallen into an unusual but works-for-all-of-us situation. Maria, always the good Catholic opposed to artificial birth control, devised a birth control method of her own for when she wasn't in the mood: she'd send her horny husband to Mason's for some "de-horrification."

Chapter Eight

"So, you promised to tell me about your mysterious past sometime," I said with a smile. "How about right now?"

Dayrn looked at me, then lifted the beer to his mouth. "You really to hear about when I was nineteen and young, dumb and full of cum?" He laughed as I nodded. "The things that I did when I was younger just shock the crap out of me now. Other then a few circle jerks when I was in my early teens I was truly inexperienced. I was mildly curious but had been working so many hours with my job that I could hardly keep up with my girlfriend who had finally broke it off. I was a wrecker driver, and the tow truck business was keeping me busy.

It had been storming and I had been trying to end it for the night when I took a desperate call for a lock out on a secluded road going out of town. The driver had locked his keys in the car and was anxious to get back inside. He did not have the entire fee, but I decided to help him out anyways. He had walked almost two kilometres to call so I felt bad for him and told him I would pick him up at the payphone on the way to the car so that he didn't need to walk in the rain.

When I pulled up at that gas station where he'd used the phone, he certainly looked pitiful. He was about five eleven, one fifty, and was wearing a parka that was soaked right through. It was hard to tell but I thought maybe his hair was dark blond and looked darker because it was soaking wet. This was in contrast to my bright blond hair no matter how wet it was.

He looked as if he had been crying, his eyes were very red. I introduced my self, and in the deepest voice I had ever heard he told me his name was Marvin, to call him "Marvin" and "thank you." As we waited for a light he told me that he was new to town, drove forty-five

"

minutes each way and was on his way home from working his tenth day of overtime when he locked the keys in the car. He said that he basically had no life other then work. I told him that I had the same problem.

I put on the heat and tried to dry him up some. I told him to pull off the parka and lay it across the dash to start drying. I turned on the map light so he could see what he was doing. When he pulled off the jacket, he pulled off his t-shirt also. He not only had the tightest six pack I had ever seen, but his nipples were sticking out and hard from being cold. He had really light hair mid way down his chest that trailed into his pants. He noticed I was watching.

"I can't help the titty hard-on, I'm freezing."

I replied that I had the affect on women, but who knew that I had that power over men too. He just gave me a weak giggle.

As I pulled up to his car it had almost stopped raining and he rolled down the truck window to wring the water out of his shirt. Even with it somewhat dark, the light made him look completely white and pale. Almost vulnerable, I told him to stay put and dry up.

It only took me a moment to unlock the car door. I retrieved the key and went back to my truck. I asked him how in the world he had locked his keys in his vehicle way out here.

He gave me a somewhat sheepish look as he replied. "I was trying to hurry and get home, and with all of the rain I really had to go to the bathroom. I pulled over, slid to the passenger side, climbed out and left the door open. I stepped away from the car to take a whiz. I didn't realize how slippery the grass was and slipped, pushing the door shut..."

I though maybe he was going to start crying when he burst into laughter. I couldn't help it and started laughing too.

I took his information and was writing his receipt when a cop pulled up shining a light into the truck. I can only imagine how that looked; a tow truck parked *behind* a car on this secluded road, and the passenger from the car was sitting next to me half naked.

The officer asked if everything was alright. We explained what had happened and I did my best not to start laughing again. He informed us that the bridge up ahead was closed off, and that when we left there was just enough room up ahead to turn around. I thanked him and he left. We both started laughing again.

Marvin was in panic, because he did not know another way home. He gathered up his clothes and had just opened the door when it started raining again. "Thank you again, I appreciate it," and before I could say anything he had fled to his vehicle.

I pulled around him and down the street, turned around and was almost back to his car when I noticed that he had not moved. I pulled over and rolled down my window.

"Was my car running when you took the keys out?" Marvin said, looking even more pitiful.

"Nope," I told him, "it wasn't."

"Shit. That means I've run out of gas or something." He just started crying then.

I had no idea what to do, so I ordered him back into the truck. Once inside, I helped him pull the parka back off. He had not put the t-shirt back on and as expected his nipples were standing at full attention.

I turned the truck around again, this time backing up to it to tow it away. Between sobs Marvin told me that he didn't have any more money and I told him not to worry about it. I told him he could come to my house for the night, wash his clothes and just go to work from there. He was still crying but he seemed to be getting better. I told him to just work on getting dry before he became sick.

I flipped on the work lights and climbed out of the truck. It took me a while to hook up the car, the entire time I was thinking about the half naked man in my truck. I looked back once and he seemed to have recovered some, and looked like he was changing the radio stations. I was afraid that he would notice the tent in my pants, so I kept my back to the truck the best I could. It was starting to pour now and I was glad to be back in the truck with its steamed over windows.

I was surprised that Marvin had not quit crying, but had slowed to a sob. I was more shocked to see that he had stripped off his shoes, socks and pants. He was sitting there in just his boxers, and they also looked soaked. I told him that we would sit there a few minutes until the storm passed before I tried to pull away. Little did I know that the storm was only going to get worse.

It was practically hot in the cab, so I struggled to remove my rain coat. I pulled my shirt up to wipe the rain from my hair and face.

Marvin stopped crying immediately as he looked at me.

"What?" I said.

"I can see that you now have the titty hard-on. I guess I have that affect on men too?" He started laughing.

"Actually, my nipples stick out like that all the time. They are not hard yet." I told him. He did not believe me so without thinking I said "feel them and see!" I was suddenly uncomfortable as he reached across and cupped my breast, then put my nipple between his index finger and thumb like he was going to pinch it. He kept his hand there for a long time and there was an awkward silence. Just then there was a flash of light and thunder struck close to the truck.

Marvin pulled away and started apologizing.

To lighten the mood I said "I told you that I had that affect on both men and women". We started to laugh and the atmosphere lightened.

"It doesn't take much to excite me, it's been so long that even thinking about my hand can get me excited" he said, then "I am just so busy that I never get to have any fun."

I told him that I know the feeling.

"I know it sounds bad, but I take it where I can get it. Even if it's with a guy."

I was speechless.

We sat there for a few minutes when he finally said "Did I upset or scare you?"

I didn't reply right away, and he was looking nervous. Thunder shook the truck again. "No."

"Then why did you get so quiet?" he asked.

"If I had known, I would never have made those comments earlier."

He seemed relieved. I told him that I liked girls, and other then a circle jerk a long time ago, I had no interest in boys up to now. My mind was racing now, and my pants started to tent again.

"Something must excite you; I saw that you were sporting a totem while you were hooking up the car." As I looked over he gently slid his hands into his boxers. He cupped his package and said "Sometimes you have to take it where you can get it."

My heart was racing, and I had no idea what to do. I continued to watch him, the dash lights just giving me enough light to see that he was now stroking himself with his member pointed down. I couldn't stand the pressure anymore and shifted to adjust my own erection, my hands in my pants to move it to the side.

"That's it, make yourself more comfortable."

It was incredulous. A few minutes ago he was a bawling baby but now he seemed as smooth as ever. Lightning stuck close by and the truck shook. Marvin practically jumped into my lap. He apologized and slid away from me, but not all the way back to where he started either. He was closer then before.

I don't know if it was the heat, or the smell of man in the truck with the heat going but I was more tuned on then ever. He pulled his boxers down enough to release his prick. It was amazing from what I could tell. A solid eight inches cut. You could see the outline when lightning stuck and its profile from the dash lights. He kept watching me watching him. I was starting to hurt as my dick struggled to be released.

In one fluid movement Marvin reached over and stroked me through my jeans. I just sat there and froze, moving to look straight ahead, afraid I was going to burst at any second. He slid closer to me in the seat, his bare legs on each side of the hump in the floor.

Slowly he placed his thumb into my jeans and hooked under my boxers. I felt it brush against my pubic hair and fought the urge to move. As if they had a quick release, he had the belt unbuckled and snap undone. The zipper sort of opened by itself and my boxers spilled out with my dick pushing straight up. He immediately placed his hand inside, moving his fingers through my pubes, going in a circular motion, just barely touching me, almost as if he was teasing. He placed his hand around my manhood, moving slowly to the base where he cupped my balls. Involuntarily I bucked forward, unable to hold still, overpowered with the ecstasy. He slid both boxers and jeans down so when I returned to the seat I could feel the vinyl against my bare ass.

Marvin leaned in closer, and used his right hand to slow stroke me, our faces almost touching. I could feel his breath on my face and I could not help but to stare deeply into his eyes. I am not sure what I saw, peace, calmness, or lust. Before I could even give it a second thought, he squeezed on my nuts again, but this time when I bucked forward he kissed me. At first it was just our lips touching, but he removed his hold and placed both hands on either side of my face, pulling me closer to him. The kissing became more frantic and his tongue darted deep into my mouth.

What seemed like just a few moments must have been a long time, and slowly he moved his kissing to my neck. I have no idea what came over me but I wrapped my hand into his hair and forced him tighter to my neck. He became more aggressive as his hands traveled up my shirt pinching on my nipples and his kissing turned to sucking and gentle biting. I had never been this hard before and was in heaven.

Thunder and lightning struck close by, and he paused for a moment. The storm had increased around us and for a brief moment I had the thought we should move to safety.

Before I could even vocalize my concern he had moved to my lap, placing the tip of my manhood into his mouth, his hands rubbing my thighs. He swirled his tongue around the head until I thought I couldn't stand it any longer. He took me deeper into his mouth, his tongue now stroking my shaft. He moved one hand to my balls, the other to my shaft, stroking every so slowly. I could not help but moan. I felt so wet, as his saliva was everywhere, dripping onto my balls and mixing with my hair.

He was back to the head, his tongue bringing me close to the edge when he retuned to the shaft. This time he took the whole length, I could feel his tongue at the top of my balls and felt them tighten. I was just about to explode when he pulled off of me and began to lick my balls. I was already about to shoot and he had found another way to wind me tighter. He looked up at me and our eyes met. He just stopped for a moment and slowly moved up to face me. Our mouths met again and the frantic kissing resumed. He climbed onto my lap, straddling either side and faced the rear. He had honked the horn once and I was shocked that we both fit. I felt his bare ass and crotch with my hard dick and fought to keep control.

Marvin slid off my shirt and started to kiss and bite on my nipples for a moment. Short on breath, he managed to gasp: "I need some help."

I looked at him puzzled when he lifted himself up, one hand on the door, the other behind him on the wheel, moving his ass backwards over my swollen dick. I knew then what he needed help with.

I reach down and slowly guided my dick to where I thought the opening of his ass was. He moved front to back as if trying to help and shook his head. "No, that's not it."

I placed both hands between our legs, palms up and took a good feel of his cheeks. They were muscular and hairy and excited me even more. I slowly explored into his crack until I found his hairy man hole and pulled him forward, guiding my rod to the hole. My dick was still so wet that I used some of his mouth juices to rub the entrance of his hole. This time it was his turn to moan. With the tip of my dick at the hole, he slowly lowered himself just a little, and by his face he seemed to be in concentration. We stayed like that a few moments when he slid down a little more. This time he seemed to be in a bit of pain and tried to pull back up and lost hold on the wheel and dropped another couple of inches. He screamed out and I immediately reached forward trying to hold him up, gently pushing up. I noticed that the storm was increasing, and was already worse then any storm I had been in.

He regained his hold on the wheel. "Ok, move your hands." Almost immediately he lowered himself more, pausing for another moment, and then sat completely on my dick. Again, I just about lost it. With his hands free now he leaned forward and kissed me, His hands on either side of me. As if on cue, lightning stuck and the thunder shook the truck. Immediately Marvin lifted up and then back down moaning as we kissed. With the next set of mother natures events he lifted up then back down, moaning again. As the thunder increased so did his thrusting. Our kissing became less accurate and he moved to my neck.

Finally I was oblivious to the storm and was concentrating on not blowing my load but his moaning had now become screaming. Faster and faster. He lifted so high that I though I would slip out. He was going faster and faster. Now it was my turn for screaming when I noticed that he wasn't lifting as high and his thrusting became more frantic. I could not hold back any longer and involuntarily thrust forward pushing him onto the steering wheel making the deepest thrust yet. As if on cue, he shot all over my chest and the long streams of cum hit my face and window behind me. We stayed like that for a moment, and as my senses returned I heard the horn blaring. Almost immediately we started laughing.

As he climbed off of me, he kissed me once again. "Are you okay?"

I could only smile back at him. We used his wet t-shirt—it was practically dry at this point—to clean ourselves up. The storm was still going strong but I was also afraid that policeman would come back so we continued at my house. Marvin didn't bother to put any of his clothes back on, so by the time we got home I was hard and ready to go again. I wasn't even stressed that the neighbours might see him streak across the yard.

Chapter Nine

"Wow, Daryn, that's a pretty hot encounter," I told him.

He just gave me a shrug. "Things happen...course, that was the only time *anything* like *that* happened to me."

I handed him a fresh beer. "So you took him back to your place?"

"Yeah." Daryn nodded.

My naked guest and I finally made it inside the house I was renting, and the storm was still raging outside. We both stood there in the foyer, dripping water onto the floor. There seemed no need to turn on a light. I was completely soaked through now, and Marvin didn't have on a single piece of clothing. He was holding them in a bunch, still dripping water onto the entryway.

We had just come back from towing his car and I had invited him to stay the night. Regardless of how we had played, the sight of this naked man next to me on the ride here, and then when he streaked across my yard from the driveway had me all ready to go again. I was almost not able to get the key in the door just to get inside.

Now that we were inside and safe from the roaring storm outside, I just stood there and stared at him. And Marvin was looking back at me. We were like frozen, just watching each other. Every flash of lightning illuminated his body. He was about five eleven, one sixty pounds. His hair looked dark but I knew he had dark blond hair. I tried to see the hair on his chest and crotch but in the next flash of light his profile showed me his hairy ass and legs. I tried to look at his crotch to get a good view of his nice thick cock but when I looked down he did not appear as excited as I was. "Are you all right, Marvin?" I finally asked him.

"I'm fine. Just a little cold, that's all."

Of course, I always kept the place a little cooler and being preoccupied I had not noticed the temperature. Immediately I moved forward into the house, straight to the bathroom and flipped on the light. I grabbed a couple of towels and headed back to my guest.

Marvin accepted the towel. "Thanks." He wrapped it around his waist.

The bathroom light bled out into my living room and it also partially lit the foyer. We had been in the dark most of the evening, in the storm, in the rain and in my truck. I was finally able to get a better view of this man. I could not help myself and reached out a hand to cup one of his ass cheeks.

He just smiled a little as he dried himself off.

"I tend to keep the house on the cool side cause I like it that way," I told him. "I'm not here all that much so why bother heating it?"

"I can see your point."

"The bathroom is there. You should go and take a shower to warm yourself back up."

"Good idea."

"You go ahead first, Daryn. Just point me in the direction of your washing machine." He was bending over to pick up his belongings and I had to fight the urge to grab his waist and pull him to my crotch. After all of the heat and the intensity just a while before, he did not seem all that interested now. I was not being rejected actually, but it sure felt that way.

I turned in a huff and pointed across the living room to a dark doorway. "The kitchen is there; you will find the washer and dryer behind the door." I stomped away to the bathroom, shutting the door. I immediately realized that he was left in the dark. I stripped off my damp clothes, turned on the water, and climbed into the shower shutting the glass door. I resisted the urge to stroke myself and concentrated on getting myself clean. I paid special attention to my dick; the process did not even arouse me. My erection had finally subsided, the water seemed to sober me and changed my mood. When I had finished, I climbed out, dried off and realized that I had not brought any clothes into the bathroom with me. I wrapped the towel around my waist and opened the door to leave.

Marvin was standing in the hallway, right in front of the door, with nothing on, holding one of the towels in his hand. He looked at me, saw that I had the towel wrapped around my waist, and quickly used his towel to do the same. "I thought maybe I would throw your wet clothes in with mine."

"I will get it; you can get in the shower." I turned and picked up my wet clothes from the floor. Marvin had stepped into the bathroom with me and I had to turn sideways to pass him out into the hall. I continued into the kitchen and tossed my clothes into the washer and started it. Almost immediately I heard Marvin howl, the water had probably scalded him. I ran back through the house.

Marvin had left the bathroom door open, and about the time I turned the corner he had figured out how to adjust the temperature and was back to washing himself. I stayed in the shadows of the living room, watching.

He had shampoo in his hair, and was using the soap on his dick and balls. I immediately started to get an erection again. He stood in the stream of water to rinse his front and used the bar of soap on his rear. He was very soapy and set the bar on the ledge. I could only see the side view but it appeared that he was fingering himself. Squatted a little, leaning forward into the water, rinsing his hair but keeping his hand and finger going. I almost shot another load watching. Suddenly he stopped, stood up straight and looked my way. When he didn't see me he just finished rinsing off, climbed out and towelled off. He stepped out of my view next to the sink, but when he backed up, he had the towel wrapped around him.

I knew he would be coming out soon. The storm outside was going full force and as I bolted across the hall to my bedroom the lightning lit up the hall. I was afraid of being seen so I rushed in and turned on the TV leaving the door cracked and the lights off. I laid across the end of the bed with the towel still on, and the remote in my hand.

Marvin came to the door and knocked.

I just tilted my head, leaving my body facing the TV; I noticed it was completely dark so he must have shut off the bathroom light. "Come in."

Marvin walked in, and just stood near the door.

"There's food in the fridge if you're hungry," I told him. "There is a blanket in the hall closet if you want to sleep on the couch, or there is another bedroom down the hall. Just make yourself comfortable."

"How could I be any more comfortable? I'm running around in just a fluffy towel?" He half laughed.

"I'm sorry. I usually sleep in the nude, wasn't thinking about you. I have all kinds of shorts and stuff in that dresser." I pointed to the one right at my feet, next to the bed. As he crossed the room I could see that his towel had a bulge. He was still hard!

Marvin started to go through the drawers, looking for something to wear, pulling things out and holding them to the side in the light of the television.

"There are t-shirts in the bottom drawer."

"So where do you prefer I sleep?" he asked, not looking up at me.

I almost blurted out that he should sleep in the bed with me, but held my tongue.

He had found a pair that he liked, a pair of cotton running shorts when he turned to face me. He crossed in front of the bed, right past me. I knew that he had to be able to see my erection. "I thought I would just sleep with you." He dropped the towel to put on the shorts and his full eight inches was so near my face I could smell the soap.

As if on cue, the power went out and the television grew dark.

There was an awkward moment when I could not see a thing and had no clue what to do.

The silence was stifling as I struggled for my eyes to adjust to the darkness. Then more lightning flashed and I could see his dick was sticking straight out in front of him. Before I could figure out what to do next, Marvin took control.

Immediately I could feel the warmth from his body as he moved his dick right before my face. Though he had just taken a shower I could definitely smell his man scent mixed with the soap, and it made me even hotter. I had hardly ever touched another man before this—a few wild groping sessions in the backseat of a car, or a quick blow-job—and as I contemplated my next move, Marvin made it for me.

He moved closer and the head of his dick was now touching my lips. He moved his shaft up and down, over and over the outside of my mouth. The smell was driving me insane, his head felt spongy. I felt a drop of precum when he started moving very slow and before I knew it, I opened my mouth.

At first I had just the tip of his head, and closed my mouth around it. I started to move my tongue around the slit and with gentle sucking I was trying to get more precum. It had a slight sweet but salty taste, not at all what I had expected. I was also surprised at how spongy his cut cock-head was. Within moments I had moved up to swirling my tongue around the shaft as he moaned his approval to me.

I immediately rolled off the bed and kneeled before him, removing my towel, taking even more of his shaft into my mouth. I now had about three inches of it inside and was able to work the underside of his dick with no problem.

Thunder struck, shaking the house.

I kept working the underside and moving to the head to swirl around a few times. Marvin placed his hands on my head and started to withdrawal and push back in, fucking my mouth. He picked up speed and started to shove further and further into my throat. I took about another inch when my gag reflex took over and I gagged a little. I tried to push him back a little but he held on. I placed my hand on his shaft so that I could control how deep he was pumping, he never slowed down. I used my other hand to explore his balls. I could feel them moving upwards and Marvin's moaning was increasing. He kept fucking my mouth, now even faster and harder. It was all I could do to keep him from shoving it completely down my throat, I kept him back the best that I could but a couple of times he was stronger then me and I gagged a bit, but he was fully enjoying it. I felt as his balls climbed even higher and I knew it was only a matter of time. I moved my hands from his balls back and through his ass. His hairy ass and hole made me even harder.

Almost immediately he started to shoot, I pushed and he pulled out of my mouth but continued to move his hips into my face, his dick running against my face, and he continued to shoot over my face and his chest and pubic area. It was like hot lava, a taste that is hard to describe. My entire face was covered and he had shot into my hair. Eventually he slowed down and stood there out of breath. My eyes had become a bit accustomed to the darkness and I could see it on his chest.

I felt around on the floor until I found his towel. As I started to bring it to my face, he stopped me, taking the towel and wiping his chest first and crotch. I tried to take the towel from him but he pulled on my shoulder trying to get me to stand. As I stood and started to protest about not being allowed to clean up Marvin planted his lips right on mine. Our tongues were intertwined for a brief moment and we fell backward on the bed, he straddled on top. It was not the most graceful move and we both giggled for a moment.

Then we began to kiss again, and he began to lick and suck his own man-juice from my face, my forehead and then from my neck. With the smell of his cum, his body giving out heat on top of me, and the caressing of my neck it was driving me wild. I could not help but buck upwards.

Marvin moved down, licking my chest as he went south. When he reached my cock he put the entire length of the shaft completely in his mouth. I did not know if he was making a point about me not doing the same, or showing off. Either way I almost shot my second load of the night right there. The storm was raging outside again. His tongue was touching the top of my sack and I was ready to explode.

He held it there for a moment, humming and moaning, and quickly withdrew, moving directly to my balls. He licked each one covering the entire area. He then took the head back into mouth but did not do much, but seemed to spit on it making it sopping wet. He sat up and looked at me. "Mason, you have to fuck me again!"

He didn't have to tell me twice, I was ready.

Marvin moved back up and we kissed briefly as he tried to impale himself on my cock. As before I placed my hands underneath his hairy ass and tried to guide myself into his hole. When I had the head right at the hole, Marvin tried to lower himself backwards, and I entered him. Immediately he was in pain and my dick seemed to be in a bind and started to hurt. He pulled off, moaning.

"I have some lube in the drawer if that will help."

He was now curled in a ball next to me as if in pain, with his back to me. I was concerned for him, but was more worried about my dick getting inside of him. "Try it now," he said with his back still to me.

I rolled over and 'spooned' with him and he pushed backwards. I quickly found his hole again and he pushed back again, this time I entered him completely. The heat from his body and the heat from his ass pushed me to the edge. I wanted it to last so I pulled out very slowly entering only when I was sure I could handle it. I pushed forward again and then back almost completely pulling out. I continued like this, in and out, back and forth, nice and slow. I did my best to keep from blasting inside of his ass and thought of things to get my mind off of his incredibly tight ass. I tried to concentrate on the storm.

Marvin started to moan on each in stroke. My mind was racing and I reached around taking hold of his cock. It was nice and soft, almost sticky. I tried to stroke it but it only made him moan more and he started clenching harder on my dick. He had been bucking backwards so much that I was completely against the wall, each stroke was balls deep. His cock had a steady stream of precum and I had no idea how long I would last. He was practically screaming in pleasure and my dick had swollen bigger then it had ever been. Within a few strokes I was shooting deep within his has. I flung my head back so hard that I hit it on the wall but hardly noticed with his ass clenching on my dick. He continued to buck a few more stokes when I felt him shoot all over my hand and bed. I had no idea that you could still ejaculate when you were soft.

Finally he stopped and we lay there, my dick inside of him, with my arm around his waist. He took my hand and brought it to his mouth and started to lick his own cum. As if on cue, thunder struck, the power returned and the television turned on. The channel that I had been watching was signing off for the night and was playing the national anthem.

Also by Frank Sol

Novels Of The Sensual City
A Family Affair
Delivering The Goods
Divine Punishment
Good Neighbours
Just Between Friends
Landscaping, Manscaping
Titan's Cradle - A Novel of the Sensual Suns

Novels On The Prairies
Bareback Range
Return To Bareback Range
Fenced In